The Family Man

ALSO BY KELLY EADON

The Wedding Date

The Family Man

KELLY EADON

FOREVER
YOURS

New York Boston

Copyright © 2016 by Kelly Eadon
Preview from the next book by Kelly Eadon copyright © 2016 by Kelly Eadon

Cover design by Elizabeth Turner
Cover images copyright © Shutterstock
Cover copyright © 2016 by Hachette Book Group, Inc.

Forever Yours
Hachette Book Group
1290 Avenue of the Americas
New York, NY 10104
forever-romance.com
twitter.com/foreverromance

First published as an ebook and as a print on demand: July 2016

Forever Yours is an imprint of Grand Central Publishing.
The Forever Yours name and logo are trademarks of Hachette Book Group, Inc.

The publisher is not responsible for websites (or their content) that are not owned by the publisher.

The Hachette Speakers Bureau provides a wide range of authors for speaking events. To find out more, go to www.hachettespeakersbureau.com or call (866) 376-6591.

ISBNs:
978-1-4555-9398-9 (ebook)
978-1-4555-9399-6 (print on demand)

The Family Man

CHAPTER ONE

Beth Beverly adjusted the wings strapped to her back, balanced the box on her hip, and slammed the heel of her hand onto the door to the coffee house.

Thud thud thud.

Sarah would flip when she saw her costume. You were never too old to dress up for Halloween. And not the slutty bunny, slutty genie, slutty maid kind of dress up. Those costumes had their time and place, but 6:00 a.m. on a weekday wasn't one of them.

She bounced on the balls of her feet as she imagined her college friend's reaction. It was too perfect that Halloween fell on a Thursday this year. Little Ray of Sunshine had started ordering her muffins a month earlier and she always delivered on Tuesdays and Thursdays at 6:00 a.m. On Thursdays, it was Sarah who accepted the delivery, and on Tuesdays, it was her hot boss. Which was also perfect. Every week she got both a

dose of eye candy and a chance to catch up with one of her favorite people.

Her antennae swayed back and forth as she shifted impatiently on her feet. She had a lot of muffin deliveries to make
and if Sarah didn't hurry, they'd miss their weekly gab session.

The door jerked open. Griffin Hall towered over her, his
eyebrows furrowing on his perfect face.

Shit. Her heart lodged in her stomach. She swallowed hard,
her eyes taking in the dark-blond hair that curled over the corners of his ears and the few days' worth of facial hair on his
chin.

Where was Sarah? Suddenly Beth wished she'd gone with
slutty…something. Anything sexier than a bumblebee. Then
again, weren't most things sexier than a bumblebee?

"Um." Her throat was scratchy. "Muffin delivery?"

He studied her for a second, then gave a polite half smile.
"Thanks. We already have a line of people at the counter waiting for their fix." He stepped to the side and held the door
open with one sinewy arm. "Nice costume, by the way."

She arched an eyebrow as she stepped inside. "You, too.
What are you? Belmont coffee shop owner who's awake way
too early? Caffeine addict who hasn't gotten his morning jolt
yet?"

He chuckled. "Maybe a combination of the two."

Her skin tingled. A chuckle and an almost smile. She was
making progress.

"So, are you guys having a good morning?" She eased past
him and into the back prep area of the bustling coffee house.
The smell of dark-roast coffee enveloped her, causing her

mouth to water. The clamor of voices drifted from the front service area. Griffin's business was always hopping and yet she'd never seen him really smile, a fact that stymied her. After all, the business she had poured her heart and soul into had bombed catastrophically two years earlier and she still found plenty of reasons to smile.

Then again, she didn't know anything about him. Maybe his family had been lost at sea and he was the sole survivor. Or maybe he was a coffee shop owner who hated mornings. Or maybe he belonged to some weird cult that required he wear mohair underwear. Whatever it was, Griffin carried something heavy. She could sense it.

Which only made him sexier.

"Sure. Been pretty busy." His voice was a low rumble, which sent her stomach into a series of somersaults.

God, he was hot. Someday, when she had more than a few seconds to spare, she'd find a way to make him smile. Not one of those smiles that merely curved the edge of his lips. A real, soul-melting smile that radiated from inside.

Today, while she stood before him as a bumblebee, was not that day. She had a dozen deliveries to make before 8:00 a.m. Time to get moving. She'd have to catch up with Sarah another time.

She lifted the lid of the box so he could see inside. "One dozen carrot cake, one dozen lemon corn, and one dozen good old chocolate chip. Think that'll get you through?"

The corners of his eyes crinkled. "You know they'll sell out in an hour. They always do."

She shrugged. "What can I say? That's one of the hazards of

being a small business. I can only make so many muffins in a day."

One failed business per lifetime was sufficient and she was perfectly content working as a part-time baker, part-time kids' drama teacher, part-time seamstress, part-time whatever. Although, ever since she'd added Little Ray to her list of clients, she hadn't been able to keep up with demand.

"Believe me, I completely understand." His irises took on a blue hue and for the hundredth time she wondered what that meant. She scanned his forehead, cheeks, chin, jaw, eyebrows. Usually she was good at reading people, intuiting their emotional states. But with Griffin? Nothing. Nada. Zip.

She tore her eyes from him and peeked into the dining room, where people crowded around tables and waited in line. Griffin's shop was a haven for people from every walk of life: local wannabe artists, bikers, stay-at-home moms, starving actors, and high school athletes. It was something he'd fostered since he'd opened six months earlier and it was one of the things that intrigued her most about him.

When she turned back, his eyes were fixed intently on her. A fire ignited low in her stomach and she had to focus to keep her breathing steady.

Holy shit. What if her crush wasn't some unrequited, one-way kind of deal?

He met her gaze and held it. Her heart raced a million miles a minute, but her tongue was glued to the roof of her mouth. What should she do now? What should she say?

She'd never in a million years expected him to look at her

the way she knew she looked at him: like she was a cupcake and he wanted to lick the frosting off.

He was still holding her gaze when Sarah entered from the storage area.

"Beth!"

She jumped, like a child who'd been caught with her hand in the cookie jar.

Now she shows up.

Sarah blinked at her, then dissolved into laughter, grasping her sides as she heaved for breath. "Again? The bee?"

Beth's face burned. She'd forgotten she was dressed as a giant bumblebee. No wonder Griffin had been staring.

"And what are you supposed to be?" she teased.

Sarah wore black tights, an orange dress and a green headband that clashed with her purple hair.

Sarah folded her into a hug. "I'm a pumpkin. We can't all be as awesome as you and fit into clothes from freshman year."

"Eh." Beth's face grew even hotter. "I don't know that anyone would call this clothes." Sarah released her, and Beth waved at her torso, which was enveloped in yellow and black stripes. Who cared what the fashion police said? Horizontal stripes would come back in eventually.

Sarah hooked an elbow through hers. "So, what kind of goodies did you bring for us today?"

Beth always made sure to feed the staff. After all, sugar was happiness.

"I haven't unloaded them yet. Come see." She glanced over her shoulder. "Griffin, you want to join us? I don't know if Sarah can be trusted to escort them safely inside."

Today's baked goods had been made specifically with him in mind.

"I'd follow you a lot farther than the parking lot for treats," he said. The left side of his mouth quirked up and her pulse sped. She was getting closer to that elusive real smile.

He opened the door and held it while Sarah and Beth walked through. As Beth passed him she caught a whiff of coffee and caramel and something manly and musky. Her heart thumped.

Sarah led the way across the parking lot to the van, which Beth had bought when she'd opened the stained-glass studio. They'd made custom stained glass and sold it in a storefront, but had also offered a delivery option. When that went out of business she'd had to find a way to repurpose the van.

"So Griff, what's May going to be for Halloween?" Sarah called out.

Beth's stomach wrenched. *A daughter.* He had a daughter? Her chest grew tight. She really should have worked up the nerve to pump Sarah for more of his personal details before she'd fallen so far into like. Or lust. This crush seemed to have a healthy dose of both. At least she'd been stealthy enough to ascertain from Sarah that he was single.

Daughters were…serious. And serious wasn't her forte.

"She's dressing as a fairy princess cat. That was an interesting shopping trip to the costume store." Griffin's voice hummed with amusement.

She grinned. May sounded like her kind of kid.

She reached for the handle to the van's door, which creaked as she tried to pry it open. Poor Martha, as she thought of her van, had seen a lot of use over the years and wasn't getting any younger.

"Need some help?" Griffin's arm brushed against hers, making her skin sing with awareness.

She abruptly stepped back from the door. "Um, sure. Just be careful with Martha. She's getting up there and she requires a delicate touch sometimes."

He raised an eyebrow. "Martha, eh?"

"Like Martha Stewart. The Hostess with the Mostest. Hostess cupcakes. Baking. Maybe you have to be drunk, but it seemed fitting when I thought of it." She and her friends Kate and Ryan had once gotten drunk during a snowstorm and brainstormed stupid names for their businesses. Ryan's recording label was named Hungry Hippo, Beth's van was Martha, and none of them could look at a bottle of Jack Daniels ever again.

Plus, renaming the van had made the bankruptcy sting a tiny bit less.

"I like it." His mouth lifted into a real, genuine smile and her skin broke into goose bumps. With a pointed look her way, he eased the door open. She ducked her head inside the van to grab a small box, which she shoved into Griffin's hands. Her stomach seemed to have launched into a full-scale fireworks display.

He grinned and arched an eyebrow as he held a finger out to her, a smattering of silver and purple sparkles flecking the surface.

She fought the urge to snort with laughter as she racked her brain. Glitter? It had to be left over from the balloons she'd decorated with her children's theater class last week. Or maybe it was from that dress she'd found at the thrift shop. Either way, there were certain things she'd never outgrow, and glitter was definitely one of them. Glitter *and* costumes.

She leaned toward him and whispered, as if she were sharing a secret. "I don't ask where Martha goes or what she does at night. I try not to pry into her private life."

He laughed, a low rumble. "Probably a good plan."

Mentally she patted herself on the back. A real smile and a laugh. And they hadn't even gotten to the contents of the box yet.

"What did you bring us?" Sarah snatched it from Griffin's hand.

"Lemon bars. I found some Meyer lemons at the store the other day." By "found" she meant she'd hunted through four local supermarkets until she'd located the perfect ones. It was imperative that these particular lemon bars be the best she'd ever made.

Griffin's eyes snapped to her face, another smile crossing his lips. "Lemon bars are my favorite."

"Really? That's crazy." She couldn't admit that she'd already known that. Someone on his staff had let it slip and the tidbit had haunted her into lemon-hunting submission. Once she got an idea in her head, she had to create the vision or it would drive her mad.

At least, that's the excuse she was going with. The fact that Griffin was dead sexy in a rugged-logger-from-the-woods kind of way only made her challenge more imperative.

"I will never say no to a lemon bar," Sarah said and shoved

one into her mouth, sending crumbs flying from her lips. "You find a new roommate yet?"

Beth glanced at Griffin, who had extracted the box from Sarah's hands and firmly secured it under one arm. Out of Sarah's reach.

"Nah. I'm just sort of seeing." She'd crunched the numbers a million different ways, and she could afford to live by herself. At least, for now.

Her heart twinged at the idea of letting someone else move into Kate's room. She was happy her best friend was madly in love and engaged, but she missed seeing her every day. There was a certain kind of intimacy you only experienced when you saw someone at their drunkest, sleepiest, craziest, and crankiest. She wasn't sure she was ready to take that leap with someone new. What if she picked the wrong person? Kate was right; maybe she should get a dog.

"If you want, you can put a flyer up in the shop. I'll make sure it stays on the front of the bulletin board and I'll try to deter any crazies from applying," Griffin offered.

She forced a smile. She wasn't prepared to have this conversation right now, especially not with him. "I'll think about it. As long as you promise to tell anyone who looks like a serial killer that I love to blast John Philip Sousa marches first thing in the morning."

He arched an eyebrow. "A John Philip Sousa reference? I'm impressed."

Sarah placed a hand on her shoulder, dragging her attention away from Griffin. "I was asking because my cousin's looking for a place. Do you want me to give her your info?"

Sarah had good taste in people, but after living with her best friend she couldn't live with just anyone. "If I decide to get a roommate, you're the first person I'll call. I promise."

She glanced back at Griffin, whose eyes had darkened. The back of her neck prickled. When had her hard-earned smile disappeared? And why?

She checked her watch, and her heart lurched. Almost six thirty. She and Martha had better get back to their regularly scheduled deliveries.

"I'll see you guys next week. Get ready for some exciting new muffin flavors! I've been experimenting." That was another reason she loved Little Ray of Sunshine. They sold whatever muffins she brought them, no questions asked. They'd even managed to sell out of her chipotle chocolate.

"Thanks for the lemon squares. I'll make sure everyone else gets one, including May. She'll love them. And I'll look forward to seeing you Tuesday." His voice was warm, but his expression had returned to unreadable.

"Anytime." She winked and climbed into the van. She'd never been one to back away from a challenge. Daughter or not, she couldn't help but be excited to earn another of his smiles on Tuesday.

* * *

Griffin stared after the van as it drove from the parking lot, willing himself to look away. He had things to do. Coffee to make, customers to serve, employees to supervise. And yet all he could think about was Beth. Her short, curly hair and the way her eyes had danced as her pink lips formed the words "lemon squares." Adrenaline shot through his veins, the way it had whenever he'd stepped onto a stage in front of a crowd of people.

A lump formed in his throat. That rush of energy was one of the few things he missed about his life as a professional musician. It hadn't been hard to say goodbye to living on the road or squabbling with his bandmates. The lifestyle had never been for him, and it was almost a relief when the band broke up. But the music? There were moments when he missed writing and performing so acutely that his chest ached.

He pushed the thought away.

No regrets. The judge had granted him full custody of Mabel. Leaving the music business had been worth it.

"Earth to Griffin." Sarah waved a hand in front of his face, jerking him back to the present. "Where are you taking Mabel trick-or-treating tonight?" she asked.

He turned back in the direction of the store.

"We're doing the trick-or-treat thing at the elementary school." Another parent from the preschool had offered to take her, but he wanted to do it himself.

He clenched his fists. *Mabel is happy. Mabel will be happy.* His daughter would grow up normal, emotionally healthy, happy, and unscarred. These days he'd probably settle for minimally scarred. Raising a kid could be damn hard, especially when you were doing it alone.

"Sounds fun. Is that why you decided to open with me today? So you could get out of here early?" Sarah fell into step beside him as they crossed the parking lot.

"Huh? Oh. Yeah." Sarah didn't need to know the way his mind replayed Beth's smile all day, every day.

Which brought him back to something she'd said. Something he needed to discuss with Sarah. He stopped abruptly.

Sarah took a few steps past him, then turned, her brows furrowed. "You okay? What's up?"

His gut tightened. He had to do this. It had to be said.

He put a hand on her shoulder. "I know you want to help your cousin, but you can't move her in with Beth."

His relationship with Sarah wasn't the typical boss-employee relationship. She was one of the few friends he had in Belmont and one of the fewer people he trusted to watch his daughter. From day one, he'd respected her tendency to say whatever she was thinking. Which is why he'd always responded in kind.

"Why not?" Her voice carried a false brightness.

Really? Was she kidding?

"Because your cousin's a convicted felon." He worked to keep his tone even, but the muscles in his jaw tensed. He didn't want to fight with Sarah; he just wanted to keep Beth safe.

He gave Sarah's shoulder a quick squeeze, then dropped his arm and yanked the door open. They'd discussed this once before, when she'd asked him to hire her cousin. And he'd flatly refused.

She shrugged as she stepped past him. "Beth doesn't care about those kinds of things. She's, you know, cool."

He gritted his teeth. His staff relied on him to be the opposite of cool, responsible even, the same way his daughter did.

That was how he kept them employed, which meant they were fed and clothed.

"She probably is. But I still think it's a bad idea." The world wasn't some magical la-la land where everything worked out. That wasn't pessimism, it was realism, and he'd had to learn the hard way.

His temple throbbed. What was it with the creative types? Had he been like this, too? Before Mabel?

Sarah sighed loudly. "Look, what do you want me to do? Mandi's my cousin. She needs a job and a place to live."

The back of his throat burned. He and Sarah were friends, but there were so many things she didn't know about him. Things he was determined to forget. How could he keep her from making the same mistakes he had?

He crossed his arms over his chest and leaned against the counter. "She sold stolen property and served two years in jail. I can't trust her to work here, and you shouldn't trust her to live with your friend. Sometimes you have to let the facts weigh more strongly than your feelings. Especially when that decision will affect people you love."

I know better than most people.

Sarah ripped open the box on the counter and began to arrange the muffins on a tray to be placed in the display case. "Mandi's boyfriend conned her into selling stolen property, and she took the fall for him because she's stupid and love is blind."

"Actions speak louder than words."

He sounded like one of those lame coffee mugs they sold at kitschy shops on the boardwalk.

He crossed the space between them and took the tray from her hands. "I get it. Trust me. I do. But you can't fix someone who doesn't want to be fixed. You can't clean up her life for her. She has to be the one who puts in the effort."

His words hung in the air.

"What am I supposed to do in the meantime? Just watch her struggle?" Tears gathered in the corners of her eyes.

He threw his free arm around her shoulder, careful not to jostle the tray of muffins he balanced in his other hand. "If you want to judge a person's character, you have to look at the things she's done in her life. That's the hard evidence. And if you don't have the hard evidence, you can't trust someone until they've proven trustworthy."

Going through the courts was a tedious nightmare, but they got things right. If Mandi had been convicted, then she was guilty.

Sarah sniffled into his shoulder. "Mandi had a crappy childhood."

He tensed. "I'm sure she did. Lots of people do. But we can't use the shit life throws at us as an excuse for making bad decisions, especially when those decisions hurt other people."

Look at him. Aside from Mabel and the coffee house, his life was nothing like he'd expected. He worked constantly, never had enough time with his daughter, and worried every damn day that he'd screw her up. The only thing that eased the web of anxiety in his chest was her smile.

And his daydreams of Beth.

He clenched his eyes shut. If she kept making lemon squares and walking ahead of him, her hips swaying hypnotically, his willpower would break. And he couldn't afford any more complications in his life.

The way he felt about Beth was dangerous. It made him feel reckless, made him want to do crazy, impulsive things. And he had Mabel to think of. No matter what, Mabel had to come first.

He opened his eyes and dropped his arm from her shoulder. They needed to get back to work.

He peered at her. "You going to be okay?"

She gave a nod. "Yup. I'll be fine. We'd better get out there before the morning rush hits."

And with that, the subject was closed to discussion.

CHAPTER TWO

Griffin surveyed Little Ray, the sense of satisfaction filling him nearly to bursting. Friday had been another busy day and the crowd had started to slow only around 3:00 p.m., which had given him just enough time to swing by the preschool to pick up Mabel. She now sat at a stool at the counter, singing for a leather-clad, fifty-something biker who sported a long, white beard. The child psychologist Griffin had consulted said Mabel needed to spend time around other adults. He was pretty sure the coffee shop crowd wasn't what she'd had in mind, but it was the best he could do.

"Then the princess climbed up the ladder," Mabel trilled, inventing the words as she went along.

Like father, like daughter. Maybe she was destined to be a musician, too.

Wisps of blond hair escaped from her braids and Griffin reminded himself to buy sturdier hair ties, the ones with the rubber grips on the inside. A mom at Mabel's preschool had said that they worked best for "active" children.

Mabel was most certainly active.

He handed a cappuccino to the next woman in line. She'd asked for low-fat milk and he'd had to explain, politely, that he didn't serve that kind of swill to his customers. Sure it was the latest fad, but people would be over it soon enough. He couldn't be remembered as serving crap coffee, otherwise how would his business survive the highs and lows? No, it was better to stick to his principles.

She took a sip. "This is the best cappuccino I've ever had."

Damn straight it was. People forgot that things tasted like cardboard when you removed any trace of fat. He carried only whole milk and people could take it or leave it. "In the morning we have really good muffins, too."

Mabel's ears perked up. "Muffins?"

The kid loved muffins. Especially Beth's mango chili ones.

"Not tonight, Mabel." It was approaching dinnertime and he should get her back to the house and fix her something that could pass for a healthy meal.

"I love muffins," she whispered to the preppy high school student seated on one side of her.

"Me, too," the girl whispered back.

Mabel turned to the biker. "Ralph, do you love muffins?"

He nodded at her and drained his coffee cup. "Absolutely. Muffins are awesome and your dad sells the best ones."

She bounced in her seat. "Ralph, do you like dinosaurs, too? I like dinosaurs but Daddy says they're not alive anymore. Did you ever meet a dinosaur?"

Ralph chuckled. "I can't say that I've had the pleasure. They lived a very, very long time ago. Before I was born, even."

This. This was why he loved Little Ray of Sunshine. Where else would so many different people have a chance to come together? Where else could his daughter learn firsthand about all of the different kinds of people there were in the world? Warmth flooded him. He needed to remember this feeling when he was awake at 2:00 a.m. reviewing purchase orders. Or when a customer stormed out because he refused to make a triple-shot, hazelnut macchiato, room temperature, with half soy, half skim milk, chocolate flakes and caramel drizzle on top.

The bell for the door jingled, and he glanced up to see his friend Ryan walk through. A redheaded woman followed him in and surveyed the shop.

Griffin grinned. Five p.m. Right on time. Ryan always stopped by for a coffee fix before he went out to see a show by one of the bands he managed.

"Hey, man." Ryan strode to the counter and clapped a hand in Griffin's.

They'd met when Griffin had booked one of Ryan's bands to play at a local art and music night. Griffin knew how hard it could be to get your big break, and he wanted to pay it forward. They'd become fast friends, discussing the music scene and swapping playlists.

"Hey. Thanks for the tip the other day. I've been listening to Lucy Dacus nonstop. She's got a great voice."

Ryan's eyes lit up. "I know, right? I saw her open at a show a few weeks ago and her lyrics have been haunting me ever since. She's brilliant. I wish I'd found her and signed her first, but she made it as a *Rolling Stone* top ten, and I think she's going to explode this year."

A brief flash of déjà vu sneaked up on Griffin. Rolling Stone *top ten*. He remembered the year his band, Thorny Lemon, had been featured as number six. Funny how times changed.

Luckily, Ryan didn't seem to notice his momentary spaceout. Which was one of the reasons Griffin liked him. Ryan knew exactly who he was, knew how popular Thorny Lemon had been and how abruptly they'd split up. But he'd never once asked about it. He simply accepted Griffin for who he was now, today.

Griffin pulled a cup to prepare Ryan's usual order. Café americano, with an extra shot of espresso. The guy was almost as much of a caffeine addict as he was himself.

"What can I get for your friend?" He nodded toward the redhead, who stood by the door, her eyes fixed on her phone.

"Ivy? She'll have a nonfat cappuccino." Ryan reached into his pocket, then slid something across the counter. When he lifted his hand, he revealed a large, black spider.

Griffin jumped. It took him a second to process the fact that the spider wasn't moving. "What the hell?"

Ryan leaned forward and grinned, his eyes gleaming. "Can you sneak this into her cup?"

Griffin grimaced. "How's she even going to know it's in there?"

"When she finishes her cappuccino she'll hear the rattling, take off the lid and find the bug!"

He groaned. "You've put entirely too much thought and planning into this."

"Trust me, I do this kind of thing all the time."

Ryan and his pranks. How did he get so many women when he pulled crap like that? Or maybe that explained why he came into Little Ray with a new date every weekend. None of them stuck around for a second spider.

Reluctantly, Griffin grabbed the bug off the counter. "Besides, you know I don't have the nonfat shit."

"I know, but nobody has to tell her that, right?" Ryan winked.

He shrugged. While he didn't necessarily believe in lying, a little omission could be for the greater good. Preserving coffee integrity was definitely a worthy cause and nonfat was an abomination to cappuccinos everywhere.

"So who are you going to see tonight?" The pitcher of milk spluttered as he submerged it under the steamer.

"Mustachio the Monkey, out in Stonyfield. You want to come with?"

Sarah sidled up beside Griffin and leaned on the counter. "Oh, you should. A bunch of us are going. We can carpool if you want."

He sighed and rolled his shoulders, trying to ease the knots in his back. "Can't. Don't have a sitter."

Another harmless lie. Much as he missed the nightlife and having friends outside of work, that wasn't for him anymore. Loud concerts at the Black Cat and shooting whiskey until the sun rose couldn't hold a candle to having his baby girl fall asleep in his arms. Or her pleas for just one more story.

Besides, he cringed to remember how his pre-Mabel lifestyle had been portrayed by Angela's parents in court. Nope, he was done with that life for good.

"My cousin could probably do it," Sarah volunteered.

His stomach clenched. The jailbird? No way. He'd never leave Mabel with someone he didn't know, much less a convicted felon.

Sarah must have read the look on his face because she sighed impatiently. "Not Mandi. The one who runs a day care."

His jaw remained tense. Tonight was his time with Mabel, to tell her stories and tuck her into bed. It was the single best part of his day. "That's nice of you to offer, but I promised her Daddy and daughter time."

Sarah placed a hand on his arm. "You're the best dad, you know that?"

His chest grew tight. God, he hoped that was true. "Not the best, but I'm trying."

Sarah squeezed his arm tighter. "The very fucking best. I know it."

Ryan rolled his eyes and drummed his fingers on the countertop. "This is a really sweet moment and all, but I need to get moving. Give me a call if you change your mind, Griffin."

Griffin poured the steamed milk into the cappuccino, topped it off with froth and snapped a lid on top. Then, with Ryan's view blocked by the cappuccino machine, he slipped the spider into Ryan's espresso and snapped another lid on top. It was just a shame he wouldn't get to see the look on Ryan's face when he discovered it.

He placed the cups on the counter. "Your coffee, sir."

"Thanks. Oh, and I brought you this." Ryan placed a thumb drive on the counter, then grabbed the cups, one in each hand.

"Demo?" He eyed it expectantly.

"A mix I thought you might like. Good for the car ride home. Let me know what you think."

"Awesome, thanks, man." He plucked it off the counter and slid it into his jeans' pocket.

Ryan raised a hand goodbye and sidled out the door, his newest lady friend in tow.

Sarah nudged him. "You can take off, you know. I have things here covered."

"Are you sure?" Technically his shift as manager was supposed to end at three, but they'd been slammed all day and he hadn't wanted to leave them short staffed.

She reached for a rag and began to wipe the counter. "Yup. You do need to hire someone, though. Someone with closing privileges."

He raked a hand through his hair. He knew. Over the last six months Little Ray's business had grown exponentially, far beyond what he'd predicted in his business plans. It was a good problem to have and yet he didn't have the energy to deal with it today.

"Noted. I'll see you tomorrow. And thanks."

Griffin turned his attention to Mabel. "All right Mabel, say goodbye to your friends, please." She knew more of the customers' names than he did and he had a suspicion that most of the afternoon crowd stopped by specifically to see her.

She pouted but jumped off the stool and shuffled to a nearby table. "Goodbye, Mary, goodbye, Sam, goodbye, Thunder…"

Griffin glanced at the grizzled old man who was hunched over a cup he was fairly certain contained a good dose of whiskey. Was that really the guy's name?

The man grunted back at Mabel with a smile. Huh. Maybe his name was Thunder.

"Daddy!" Mabel's voice reverberated through the noisy coffee shop.

He gave her a pointed look. "I'm coming. What did I say about inside voices?"

"Inside voices are overrated!" She hadn't adjusted her volume, and the customers in the shop burst into laughter, which made her beam triumphantly in his direction. Where had she learned the word "overrated"? Did she even know what it meant?

He couldn't help himself. A low laugh escaped him. So much for not encouraging bad behavior. His girl had a future as an actress or a comedian. Definitely something that involved the stage.

His brain pinged with a faint memory. Crap. Kid theater classes started in a few days and he'd totally forgotten to sign her up. Some dad he was. He'd have to check the website when she went to bed and pray they still had a spot open.

He sighed, crossed the room to Mabel and scooped her up. She wrapped her arms around his neck and laid her head on his shoulder. The scent of her baby shampoo wafted in the air.

Once he'd strapped her into her car seat, he plugged the thumb drive into his adapter. A file named For the Kid appeared on his phone screen. Maybe Ryan was a softie after all. He opened and clicked.

Kasey Musgraves filled the car with a song about biscuits. In the backseat Mabel nodded and hummed along. When it ended there were a few seconds of dead air before heavy metal began to blast: "I eat you in your face! I smash you in your face! I am a cannibal! I am a cannibal!"

He slammed on the brakes and jerked the car to the shoulder, then punched the Pause button on his phone and glanced in the rearview mirror.

His chest pounded and his heart raced. How was that a kid-appropriate song?

In the backseat, Mabel was giggling. "You can't eat someone's face! They're silly, Daddy. There's no such thing as a can animal."

He breathed a sigh of relief. Freaking Ryan and his practical jokes.

* * *

Beth clutched an ice-cream cone in one hand and dug through her purse with the other. She located a few one-dollar bills and tried to shove one in the tip jar, but they scattered across the counter.

"Beth. He's not a stripper. You can't go around throwing money at people." Kate pressed her lips into a line, a sure sign she was trying not to smile.

"Says who?" Beth shot back.

Her best friend burst into laughter.

"Everyone likes tips," Beth added as she shoved the wallet back into her purse.

The teenage employee's back was to them, but by the way the tips of his ears turned red she had a feeling he'd heard the exchange.

"True. But you know who usually gets tipped in one-dollar bills?" Kate bumped the door with her hip to open it.

Beth stepped outside. "Strippers?"

Kate pointed a finger at her. "Exactly."

"And how do you know this?"

Kate shrugged. "Work."

She dropped her jaw in mock horror. "Katie Massie, did you just admit to moonlighting as a stripper?"

Then she winked. Kate had wanted to prosecute since forever, and it had taken her a while to find the right job. Beth was thrilled for her best friend.

"Be nice, or I won't let you taste my ice cream." Kate waved her cone in the air, just out of Beth's reach.

"Be careful waving that thing around." Beth waggled her eyebrows to emphasize the double meaning.

Kate dissolved into giggles, giving Beth a chance to dart forward and lick the top scoop. Then she extended her cone. Kate leaned forward and licked, leaving a decent-size dent.

It was one of the many perks of best friendship: the chance to taste multiple ice cream flavors.

"I guess we'd better enjoy these, since they'll probably never let us back in that store again."

Kate rolled her eyes. "Twenty dollars says I made his day by implying people would pay to see him naked."

Beth chuckled. "Traumatized and flattered aren't mutually exclusive. Besides, loads of people get paid in one-dollar bills, you just have a dirty mind."

"Oh yeah?" Kate fell behind her as they picked their way down a narrow path to the beach. "Name five people who get paid in single-dollar bills. Servers and food workers all count as one."

Beth paused, threw her head back and inhaled the salty sea air. Belmont was so much better in the off-season when residents didn't have to dodge a crush of out-of-town beach-goers.

"Number one, the Santa who stands outside places at Christmas and rings the bell."

Kate giggled. "The money isn't for him, you know."

Beth shrugged. "It still counts. Number two, those guys who sit on the boardwalk in the summer and play the upside-down buckets like their drums. I still think Ryan should sign them to a record deal. They're awesome."

She paused to lick her ice cream. "Number three, Girl Scouts. Last time I checked cookies are still four dollars and they only take cash or check, so I bet they get plenty of one-dollar bills."

Food-service employees got her to four, which left only one spot to fill. "Whoever owns the vending machines. I bet when they clean them out there are loads of one-dollar bills."

Kate laughed. "Well done, I'd clap but I have a hand full of ice cream. Out of all those options, I still think the ice cream scooper would rather be a stripper, though."

"And like I said, you have a dirty mind," Beth teased.

"Hey, I didn't disagree. So what was yesterday's baking project?" Kate kicked off her shoes and wiggled her toes in the sand.

"Lemon squares."

"Yeah? And who were your latest victims?" Kate knew she liked to spread cheer in the form of baked goods.

"Griffin, the guy who owns Little Ray of Sunshine downtown."

"Griffin, eh? Isn't that where Ryan buys my apology donuts?"

Beth nodded. Griffin had contracted with a few local bakers for different goods, and one of them supplied the donuts. But Sarah said her muffins always sold out the fastest.

Kate wiggled an eyebrow. "Why does he own a coffee shop named after you?"

Beth froze as she remembered the way his green eyes, with their hint of blue, had burned into her. Last night she'd lain awake, replaying the image of his shaggy hair falling across his face as he stared at her. Openly.

She shivered.

Kate stopped walking and cocked her head to the side as she examined Beth. "Spill."

That's what twenty-plus years of friendship got her. Kate could see directly into her head and vice versa.

"Drop-dead gorgeous. All muscle, kind of blondish hair, strong shoulders. Exactly the right amount of stubble." Her skin heated, and she reached to fluff her short, curly hair so it partially covered her face.

"That sounds promising."

Her stomach twisted. She'd left out the daughter part. "Maybe."

"Maybe, huh? What's his deal?"

She shrugged. "I'm not totally sure. He's on the quieter side. I know he has a daughter, but Sarah told me the other week that he isn't seeing anyone."

"Ooh, the strong silent type? And kids love you. Maybe that's your in?"

Her chest grew tight. Kids required a terrifying amount of responsibility and she was one of the least responsible people she knew. She had the bankruptcy, three part-time jobs, and a house full of half-finished craft projects to prove it.

Maybe she should leave Griffin, with his successful business and normal home life, alone.

"I think that would be weird. To involve his kid. You know?"

Kate faced her and stared into her eyes. "Yeah, you're right. I have a better idea. You should dress up as a human lemon square and invite him to lick you all over. Go straight to X-rated, no kid-friendly stuff allowed."

The laughter came bubbling out and her shoulders relaxed. Casual sex. She could do that. Plus, human lemon square sounded delicious.

"He was staring at me today…"

"Of course he was!" Kate grabbed her hand and squeezed. "So, he's dark and brooding? Like Mr. Rochester?"

Beth wrinkled her nose. She'd never loved *Jane Eyre*. It was dismal and depressing, full of pain and suffering. She was more of a fairy-tale kind of girl herself. The Disney versions, not the Brothers Grimm.

Kate examined her face. "Right. No *Jane Eyre* for you... What about *Beauty and the Beast*? He's the growling, cursed prince, and you're the one who can show him the light?"

Beth let out a low chuckle. "He's too good-looking to be the beast."

Kate winked. "Well you never know what's going on underneath that brooding expression. I think you should find out."

This sent Beth into another fit of giggles. "Oh, believe me, I want to."

Kate crunched the last bite of her cone and flopped onto the sand. They'd reached their favorite spot to watch the sunset. They'd been coming out here for sunsets since the fifth grade.

"Then we'd better start planning. We'll designate Human Lemon Square as plan A, but we need to figure out how you work your way up to it."

Beth sat cross-legged beside her. "Are you sure we should make any kind of plan without Ainsley?"

Their friend Ainsley was the queen of planning. She'd been the one who'd concocted the scheme that had thrown Kate and her fiancé, James, together, and she worked as the event planner at the Méridien hotel.

"Good point." Kate reached for her phone. "I bet we could conference-call her."

Beth put her hand on top of Kate's, stopping her. This wasn't the kind of thing you could plan. It had to happen organically. "Let's just watch the sunset for now."

The faintest orange hues were starting to streak across the sky.

Kate sighed. "All right, fine. Just remember to keep it X-rated."

Beth closed her eyes and recalled the image of Griffin in his low-slung jeans and fitted plaid shirt. Her heart rate sped.

Remembering to keep it X-rated wouldn't be a problem.

CHAPTER THREE

Beth sat next to the small blond girl at the edge of the stage, facing out at the dark, empty theater. Her children's theater class had ended thirty minutes ago, and still no sign of Mabel's parents. They both swung their feet over the edge, two sets of rhythmic *thunks* breaking the silence.

Beth held out the lump of clay in her hand, which she'd fashioned into a frog. "Guess what I made for you?"

Mabel squealed with delight. "A frog! Now guess what I made for you?"

She held out her palm, her blue lump of clay settled in the middle.

Beth examined it carefully. It was a round circle, with other round circles attached at odd angles. "A cloud?"

Mabel giggled and shook her head. "Nope! Try again!"

"A flower?"

Another giggle. "Nope!"

Beth narrowed her eyes at the blob of clay. What was it?

"Hm. You're really good at this game. Can you teach me how to be as good at guessing as you are?"

Mabel grinned wider. "In the middle is his body, and then his head, and also his ears..."

Finally, it clicked. "A teddy bear!"

"Yup!!" Mabel smashed a fist into her clay, turning it into a flat blue pancake.

Without warning, Mabel's stomach rumbled. She looked up at Beth, wide-eyed. "Did you hear my belly? She sounds angry."

Beth chuckled. "My stomach makes that noise when she's hungry, too." She paused. Where were Mabel's parents? It was the first day in a new session, and they were thirty minutes late. Had they mixed up the times or gotten stuck in traffic?

"Mabel? Do you think I should call your parents?"

The little girl pulled a pipe cleaner from the pile Beth had provided and twisted it with her small fingers.

"Well," she raised her brown eyes to meet Beth's, "I don't have a mom. She was really sick, and she didn't want to leave me, but she had to. My dad says sometimes life isn't fair."

Beth's heart squeezed painfully, and she reached an arm around the little girl to pull her closer.

"Why does everyone hug me when I say that?" Mabel's voice was muffled by the fabric of Beth's sleeve.

Beth swallowed the lump in her throat and dropped her arm. "Because it stinks. I bet you miss her."

"Sometimes." Mabel made the pipe-cleaner creation prance across the stage.

"Who normally picks you up?"

"My dad. Some people have two dads, but I have one dad and he works a lot. He's going to get me when he's done with work." The little girl smiled up at her and Beth felt suddenly lighter. Little kids were incredible. They always helped her to keep things in perspective.

"What should we do until he gets here?"

It wasn't as if she were in a hurry to get back to her empty house. Kate kept texting her links to adoptable dogs, but she couldn't summon the courage to click on them. What if she messed up and forgot to feed it or take it out? What if it got sick and she missed the symptoms? What if she fed it the wrong food or bought it the wrong leash? A dog couldn't take care of itself. It would be entirely, one hundred percent reliant on her.

"Can we do the freeze-dance game?" Mabel's request broke through her thoughts.

"Sure." She jumped down from the stage. She always used the game on the first day, to break the ice and assess the kids' motor control. If Mabel wanted to play solo, who was she to say no?

She unwrapped the cord around the boom box and plugged it in. The true freeze-dance experience required authentic equipment. Nothing but a big old boom box would do.

She was about to hit the Play button when a man's voice echoed from the entryway. "Hello? Anybody here?"

The back of her neck prickled. Why did she know that voice?

A muffled curse punctuated his loud footsteps.

"In here!" Beth called back.

"Mabel?" When he strode into the room, his blond hair disheveled and his long legs covering the distance in a few strides, Beth's mouth fell open.

Griffin. She'd thought he had a daughter. And now here he was.

"Daddy!" Mabel hurled herself at her father, who kissed the top of her head and lifted her into the air.

"I'm so sorry, Mabel. There was a mix-up at the store. You knew I was coming to get you as soon as I could, right?" There was a slight shake to his voice.

Beth was acutely aware of the blood pumping through her veins. Her spine tingled and her thoughts raced.

He's here in my theater.

He placed Mabel back on the floor and bent to admire the pipe-cleaner creation she still clutched in one hand. His shaggy hair fell, covering his eyes. The edge of a tattoo peeked from under his sleeve.

Her heart thudded louder. Guys with tattoos were her kryptonite. How had she never noticed it before?

Oh God.

Her stomach dropped. She had a raging crush on a man with a daughter. And a dead wife.

Her pulse pounded in her ears. Did that make her a bad person? She wasn't prepared for any of this.

She forced herself to look away and turn to gather her things. His life was even more complicated than she'd thought. Single dad was one thing. Grieving widower was another.

She took a deep breath and pushed her hair off her forehead.

Seducing him was out of the question. It would be too weird, too awkward, too crazy. This entire thing was crazy.

"I'm so sorry I'm late, Ms...." Griffin lifted his eyes from his daughter for the first time. His jaw dropped as his eyes widened in recognition.

She froze under the power of his gaze.

"Beth?" He broke into a wide smile. It was as soul melting as she'd expected.

Her heartbeat raced even faster.

"Hi." The word rushed out softly, like a sigh. Her brain searched for something else to say, anything. She'd spent the last few weeks conjuring possible back stories for him, but her sudden discovery of the truth left her speechless.

This was a whole lot heavier than mohair underwear.

"You work here, too?" He gestured to the empty theater.

She nodded. "Yup. I make muffins part-time, I teach acting classes for kids part-time. I'm also a seamstress part-time."

She waited for the smile on his face to falter. Grown-ups were supposed to have careers and ambitious life plans. She was all too aware of the way people frowned when they realized she had neither.

Instead he took a step closer. "That's awesome. I know how hard it can be to make a living and follow your passion. That takes guts."

The understanding in his eyes made her skin tingle. *Wow.*

The growl of Mabel's stomach punctuated the quiet of the theater. "Daddy, I'm hungry."

He tore his eyes from Beth and kneeled to his daughter's

height. "Then let's get you home and feed you some dinner. Can you get your stuff, please?"

"Okay!" The little girl bounced to the stairs leading to the stage, where she'd left her backpack.

Griffin raked a hand through his hair, and his forehead furrowed. "I'm so sorry. I promise I'm not usually late. I just got caught up…"

She waved a hand. "Really, don't worry about it. Most parents are a little late and we had fun. Besides, she told me about…um…you know, that scheduling might be tricky."

His mouth twisted and her stomach dropped. She'd said the wrong thing.

"Sorry, I didn't mean, um…I just wanted you to know that it's fine. People are late all the time. It's not a big deal."

Stop talking. You're making things worse. She pinched her lips together and willed herself to shut up.

On the stage, Mabel shuffled her feet and hummed as she danced the pipe cleaner through the air.

Griffin heaved a sigh. "Don't be sorry. You didn't do anything. I just don't like to talk about"—there was a long pause—"her mom and all of that." He reached a hand to massage the back of his neck. "Does she seem okay to you?"

The uncertainty in his eyes made Beth's chest ache. Without thinking, she stepped forward and squeezed his hand. "Mabel?"

He nodded.

"She's incredible. You should be really proud of her. She has so much confidence and curiosity and creativity."

One corner of his mouth quirked up. "You don't think I

scarred her for life tonight? Like she'll be sitting in a therapist's office twenty years from now telling them about this moment and how it ruined her childhood or something?"

His eyes danced at his own joke.

She grinned back at him. "Absolutely not. I work with a lot of kids and she's pretty well adjusted, as far as I can tell." She glanced at the little girl who was now twirling in a circle, her arms thrown wide.

"Well adjusted" might be an understatement.

He chuckled. "Yeah, she's a great kid. I can't believe my own luck sometimes."

Beth's throat constricted. Before, he'd just been devilishly good-looking. Watching him with his daughter, listening to him talk about his daughter, made her insides melt.

She cleared her throat and took a quick step backward. Griffin's life was complicated. He had responsibilities. His history was difficult. She needed to remember that when his green eyes threatened to swallow her up.

"Daddy! I'm still hungry!" Mabel raced down the stairs from the stage with her arms stretched wide like an airplane.

Griffin swooped her up and sat her on his shoulders, facing Beth. "I guess I'd better get her home. She loves to eat, just like her dad, but she especially likes your muffins."

At the mention of muffins, Mabel's eyes rounded. "You make the muffins?"

She broke into laughter. "I make the muffins for your dad's store, yes."

Mabel licked her lips. "I love the muffins. I love the mango muffins and the chocolate chip muffins and the banana muffins…"

Griffin gave a good-natured roll of his eyes. "I guess I'd better take her home and feed her. I'll see you tomorrow? For the muffin delivery?"

"Yes. I'll see you tomorrow." She'd made them before class and had left them on the counter to cool. Along with a dozen chai tea scones for the staff.

"Good." He waved.

"Bye, Beth!" Mabel, still perched on Griffin's shoulders, waved, too.

"Bye, Mabel. I'll see you next week."

Griffin was still grinning when he turned and walked to the rear of the theater.

The door swung closed behind them, leaving Beth alone in the silence. She grabbed her bags and slung them over her shoulder before she trudged outside and locked the heavy wooden door to the theater behind her.

She sighed as she imagined the empty house that awaited her. A lump formed in her throat.

She pulled out her phone and texted Ryan.

Beth: Hey, what are you up to tonight?

He responded back within seconds.

Ryan: Vibe Riot is playing at Hooligan's at nine. You in?

She paused, her fingers poised above the keys. She'd have to be up and ready to deliver muffins by five thirty the next morning.

Then she imagined herself stretched out on the sofa, eating cereal for dinner, and watching the latest *Real Housewives of somewhere or other. Lame.*

She typed.

Beth: Perfect. I'll meet you there.

* * *

Griffin lifted the covers to Mabel's chin, then tucked them in around her small form.

"One more story, please?" she begged.

He shook his head. "We already read three, remember? *Madeline, Goodnight Moon,* and *The Cat in the Hat.*"

The last was his personal favorite. Thank God, too, because this was the sixth night in a row she'd requested it. How was it that kids never got tired of the same thing, over and over?

She frowned. "But I said please."

He smoothed a hand over her hair. "You did and I appreciate that. But saying please doesn't always mean you're going to get what you want."

His mind drifted back to Beth and the way her dark eyes had watched him with Mabel at the theater. He'd been so frantic to get there and so focused on reassuring Mabel, that when he finally noticed Beth her presence nearly sucked all the air from his lungs.

It couldn't be a coincidence, her being Mabel's teacher, could it? She'd been warm and patient, kind and gentle with his daughter. Which had the potential to change everything.

Mabel sighed heavily. When he didn't react, she followed it with a loud *humph*.

He swallowed a laugh. It was one of the main rules of parenting: do not reinforce bad behavior. He'd read it in a book somewhere.

"'Night, Mabel." He leaned down and placed a kiss on her forehead.

"'Night, Daddy. I do love you, even though you only read three stories."

"Well that's good, because I love you, too." He stood and dimmed the light switch. Then he stepped into the hall, pulling the door behind him until it was open only a crack.

He took a few steps down the hall to his office–music room. He twisted the handle and stepped inside, folding himself into the computer chair.

Where he sat and stared at the computer screen, the letters and numbers blurring before his eyes.

An image of Beth with her wild, curly hair and form-fitting jeans flooded his consciousness. His heart thudded in his chest.

Funny how when Beth reassured him that Mabel was well adjusted it actually eased the knots in his stomach. He exhaled a long breath. He knew that other parents got stuck at work and were late to pick up their kids. People had faith in single mothers, but single fathers? He'd caught the doubting looks people slanted in his direction.

Not Beth. All he saw in her eyes was warmth, faith.

His heart pounded. He hadn't dated much in the last few years. It had always been too complicated to juggle father-hood, a career, and a personal life. But what if he didn't have to choose? What if there was a way to have all three?

A video chat popped open on his computer screen. Ryan.

Music pulsed in the background and lights of a club flashed over his face.

"Hey, man. One of my bands is playing at Hooligan's tonight. I figured I'd check and see if you wanted to swing by."

Griffin smiled to himself. Even though he was rarely able to go out, Ryan always invited him.

"Thanks, man. I just put Mabel to bed and I have to wake up early to open the shop tomorrow. Maybe another time?"

Every second with Mabel was precious. He wanted her to fall asleep knowing that he'd be there. She needed the certainty of knowing that she was always the top priority to her remaining parent.

"Definitely. Another time. I'll hook you up with a good babysitter. I have a friend who's awesome with kids. They worship the ground she walks on."

He gave a noncommittal nod. There weren't too many people he trusted with Mabel, which was part of the reason he didn't have much of a social life.

"Looks like a good crowd." From what he could see, there were at least a hundred people behind Ryan. It was a good turnout for a small local band on a weeknight considering they wouldn't take the stage for another hour.

"It is an awesome crowd. Great energy."

Familiar, tousled, curly hair came into view as the cell camera skewed to the side.

"Hey, Bethie!" The camera captured Ryan looping his arm around his shorter companion.

Griffin's heart thudded. Beth. Of course she was friends

with Ryan. The population of Belmont was small, especially during the off-season.

Her lips were cherry red and she wore some kind of flared top that accentuated her curves. Blood rushed below his waist and he shifted uncomfortably in his desk chair.

Holy shit. He'd never seen her like this before.

"Griffin, meet Beth! She's my favorite midget!" Ryan held the phone one-handed, which caused the phone camera to shake.

"I'm not a midget!" Beth punched him in the arm and the camera tilted further, focusing on their feet. A bright cartoon hummingbird was tattooed on her ankle, which curved down to tall, pointed, high-heeled shoes.

A bead of sweat trickled down the back of his neck. Feet. They're just feet. Who knew feet could be so sexy? No, he corrected himself. It wasn't feet in general.

Suddenly, he wished he'd hired a babysitter for the night.

The camera righted. On the screen, Beth waved at him.

"Hi Griffin! Small world, huh? Apparently we're destined to keep running into each other."

Before he knew it, he was grinning back at her. "I guess so. Next time I'll have to join you two."

She nodded. "Absolutely. I'm going to go get some drinks, but I'll see you in the morning."

Before he could say goodbye, Ryan had angled the phone's camera so it was focused back on his face.

"See you in the morning?" He lifted an eyebrow.

Griffin's face heated. "She delivers muffins to Little Ray."

Ryan chortled. "I know, I know. I just like giving you a hard time. You should have seen your face! Anyway, that's the friend I was telling you about. Best babysitter in the universe. Let me know when you want to go out and I'll send her by your place."

He was shaking his head before he even realized it. "I don't want to inconvenience her. I'll find someone and we can all go out next time."

Ryan's eyes widened, prompting Griffin to add, "With some of my staff. I'm sure we can get a good group together."

He regretted the words the moment they left his mouth. Who cared if Ryan knew he was interested in Beth?

Ryan winked. "I'm going to hold you to that. Well, have a good night. I'll catch up with you tomorrow."

The tips of Griffin's ears burned. "Yeah, bye. Have fun."

The video chat box went black, but he couldn't tear his eyes away from it. Images of Beth, her red lipstick, her hummingbird tattoo, and the curve of her hips flooded his head.

It was time to find a babysitter. And time to get a life.

CHAPTER FOUR

This morning Beth had dressed appropriately for a muffin delivery. She wore a blue fit-and-flare dress with ankle-high suede boots, which was loads better than the bumblebee costume. Her heart fluttered at the thought of Griffin, with his shaggy, blond hair falling over his green eyes.

She paused to check her reflection in the rearview mirror. Crazy hair, as usual. It had always been riotously curly but chopping it off to chin length had only made it worse. Oh well.

She hopped from the driver's seat. This was a muffin delivery, nothing else. Not that she'd say no to something else.

Go for X-rated. The memory of Kate's advice sent another flash of heat coursing through her body.

She shook her head in an attempt to clear it. *Kid. Deceased wife. Baggage. Commitments. Complications.*

Maybe if she repeated those things enough times, her hormones would fall in line.

Doubtful.

She took a deep breath, wrenched open Martha's back door and balanced the first box of muffins in her arm, carefully stacking the others on top.

When she turned, she bumped into something solid and the boxes nearly toppled to the ground. Griffin reached out a hand and gripped her upper arm, steadying her.

Her breath caught in her throat as her eyes traveled his face.

"Sorry. Are you okay? I didn't mean to scare you." His eyes were full of concern.

She swayed toward him, drawn in by his coffee scent. It should be illegal to smell so good.

Then she jerked herself upright, her cheeks going hot. "Yes. I'm not fully awake, I guess."

"Let me take those." He eased the boxes from her arms, his warm hands brushing against her bare skin. Heat pooled in her belly.

"Then I'll get the door." She quickly walked in front of him and propped it open with her hip. "Busy today?"

He smiled as he strode past her. "Not any more than usual."

He set the boxes on the counter and turned to face her, a smile playing on his lips. "Do you like coffee?"

Did she like coffee? What was she, a zombie? "Love it."

He gestured her over to a large metal table and pointed to a few sample bags of beans. "I was just about to sit down with some samples. Care to join me for a coffee tasting?"

Her heart thumped as her brain rushed to calculate. She had three more deliveries to make with Martha before 7:00 a.m. If she took twenty minutes for each delivery she could make it as long as she was out of here by... Her eyes drifted to the clock. Five minutes. She had exactly five minutes left with Griffin.

Damn.

His smile faltered. "Or I can get you a coffee for the road?"

A pang of regret hit her. "Griffin," she placed a hand on his arm, "I would love to do a coffee tasting with you, but I have a ton of deliveries to make this morning and only thirty minutes to finish them. I definitely wouldn't say no to a coffee for the road, though."

His shoulders relaxed again. "Coming right up. And I'll take a rain check on the coffee tasting. You seem like you have good taste and I'd love to borrow your palate for an hour."

She watched as he slipped into the dining room. Was that an invitation for a date? Or just a compliment? She bit her lip.

She wanted it to be a date. In spite of the fact that he had a child, he was a widower, and they technically worked together. Which only proved that she wasn't very good at making mature, adult decisions.

Griffin returned, with a to-go cup in hand. On the side he'd scrawled "Beth" in angular block letters. She found herself staring at them. Interesting. Maybe he hid an artist's creative spirit after all.

"Cappuccino. It's my special recipe. Let me know if you can guess the secret ingredient. If you guess correctly, you win a prize." He winked and her knees went weak.

Can you be my prize?

She clamped her lips together. She needed to get out of here, before she said or did something truly unprofessional.

She lifted the lid and let the coffee aroma waft over her.

"Cardamom." He'd have to do better than that to stump her.

His jaw dropped. "You didn't even taste it."

"But it is cardamom, right?"

After a pause he nodded his head. "How did you know?"

She shrugged. "I bake. I guess I'll be eagerly awaiting my prize, then?"

He chuckled, long and low. "I'll surprise you."

They stared at each other, the silence heavy between them. Then she flashed him a smile and turned to the door.

"We'll see about that," she called over her shoulder.

* * *

Griffin punched buttons on the computer screen while he whistled to himself.

An error message popped up and he hit Reset with his index finger. The screen froze, blinking at him.

He bit back his normal mutterings regarding a sledgehammer, took a deep breath and counted to ten.

Bingo.

The receipt scrolled in front of him.

"That'll be six dollars and forty-nine cents." He tilted the card reader toward the customer, who swiped his credit card through.

The computer hesitated, the word "processing" flashing across its screen.

Sarah sidled up next to him and peered at it. "Is it acting up again? I swear I'm going to beat it with my shoe."

He raised one arm in front of her, as if holding her back. "Whoa there. The computer's having a rough day. We need to be patient with it."

Sarah blinked at him. "What's going on here? Is this an episode of *Candid Camera*? Or *Body Snatchers*? Are you an alien in Griffin Hall's skin? Are you going to eat us all?"

She lifted a finger and poked tentatively at his face.

He waved her off with a laugh. "Don't be crazy."

Then he went back to whistling.

Sarah's eyes burned into him. "Holy shit. Did you finally get laid?"

He jerked his gaze up to meet hers.

"Are you nuts?" It came out as a hiss.

Little Ray was his place of business. There was no reason any of his customers needed to know about his sex life. Or in this case, lack thereof.

She examined him. "Something's going on. I can sense it. If you don't tell me, I'll find out. I'll plant bugs in the coffee shop."

"You know I can fire you, right?" His tone was matter-of-fact.

She rolled her eyes. "You can, but you won't. You're short-staffed as it is and I'm practically the only other person you have to open in the mornings and close at night."

He sighed. True enough. He really did need to hire more baristas, but, unsurprisingly, most people didn't like to wake up at the crack of dawn. And he wasn't about to degrade his business standards by hiring people who sucked. Lately, a lot of the applicants sucked.

"I'm not getting laid, okay?" He clenched his jaw and ground out the words. Maybe now she'd drop it.

Instead, Sarah grabbed his elbow and dragged him into the back.

"I'm not stupid. You're cheerful. I want to know why." She tapped her foot.

When he didn't answer she folded her arms over her chest and scanned the room. Her attention focused on a platter of muffins.

Then her gaze darted back to him. "Wait...Beth was here."

His jaw tensed. He didn't owe his employees any explanations.

A slow smile spread across her face. "I guess this means you're going to let me close the shop for you Thursday night."

He frowned. "Why would I do that?"

He'd already scheduled himself for Thursday, so he wouldn't have to pay anyone overtime. He'd pick Mabel up from Children's Theater and she'd hang out until it was time to close up.

She smirked back at him. "Beth teaches Mabel's theater class on Thursdays. She's free after. You can take her to dinner."

His pulse sped.

A date. With Beth. How long had it been since he'd had a date? Mabel and Little Ray took up every second of his day.

Mabel.

He cleared his throat. "You're forgetting Mabel. I can't bring her on a date and I'm not going to find a sitter on such short notice."

She shrugged. "Invite Beth over for dinner. After Mabel goes to sleep."

The bell on the front counter dinged, indicating the arrival of an under-caffeinated customer.

"I'll get that." She winked at him, and then sashayed through the door to the front of the shop.

He stared after her. Why hadn't he thought of it sooner?

Sarah's plan solved all of his problems. Mabel was a heavy sleeper, so he'd finally have time alone with Beth. And he wouldn't have to scramble to find a trustworthy babysitter.

He pulled his phone from his back pocket and pulled up a new text message.

> Griffin: Since you didn't have time for coffee today, how about you come over for dinner on Thursday? Mabel goes to bed at eight. Any time after that is good.

He put the phone on the metal food-prep table and drummed his fingers against its surface. What did he do now? It could be hours before she responded. He needed a distraction.

The phone vibrated and he snatched it back up.

> Beth: Sounds great. I'll be there.

Adrenaline flooded his veins. It was a date.

CHAPTER FIVE

All day Thursday her stomach was a bundle of nerves, her mind a constant loop of doubts.

He had a daughter. Anyone he dated would eventually, by association, kind of have a daughter. And she regularly forgot to water her garden boxes. She wasn't equipped to be at all, remotely responsible, for a small human.

Plus, he'd lost his wife. Did he know that she knew? Would he want her to know? Should she pretend she didn't know? Or should she just put it all out there in the open?

Kate had been no help, texting her that she should relax and be herself.

By 7:30 p.m. she'd bitten her nails down to short, ragged stubs.

Sexy. Ainsley would have had a fit.

She was standing in front of her closet, staring at her clothes when her phone rang. Kate's number flashed across the screen.

"Hello?" She flipped through the hangers of clothes for the

hundredth time. Yellow dress. Blue shirt. Green pants. They were all wrong.

"Are you ready for the big date?"

Beth's stomach did a somersault. "Well..."

She heard Kate suck in a breath. "Please tell me you're dressed and about to get in your car and drive over there."

"Well..."

Kate sighed loudly. "All right. Tell me what's going on."

Beth flopped back onto the bed. "I'm nervous."

"Nervous about what, specifically? Maybe it'll help you to say it aloud."

"There's just a lot to think about. He has a daughter and his wife is dead and I have to see him twice a week at work, more even because Mabel's in my class now." Her voice wavered.

Kate's voice, on the other hand, was firm. "Beth Beverly, a hot man asked you on a date. You want to lick him from head to toe, like a human lollipop. I don't care if he's a freaking furry, you get your ass over there. You eat dinner. You make out with him and then you report back to your best friend because she loves you."

There was silence for a long moment, before Beth burst into laughter. "A furry? Really?"

Kate giggled. "I don't know, the only things that came to mind were that and a clown. Anyway, I had a feeling this would happen. Ainsley's on the other line and I'm going to buzz her in. She'll help you figure out what to wear."

Beth exhaled. Thank God for Ainsley. If anyone could help, it was her.

There was a long beep followed by a chipper "Hello!"

"Hey, Ainsley. Um, I don't know what to wear."

"No worries, honey, I already have it figured out. Since you're going to dinner at his house, cute, dark jeans are perfect. Is your red sleeveless top with the high-lo hem clean?"

Beth flipped through the clothes in her closet until she found the shirt that matched Ainsley's description. She leaned in and sniffed the fabric. Definitely clean. "Yup!"

"Great. Wear that with the jeans and a cute pair of sandals. If your toenails are painted. Are your toenails painted?"

She slipped her feet out of her slippers. Glitter toenail polish.

"Yup!"

"Perfect. You'll be gorgeous. Send us a picture so we can admire you. And good luck!"

The tension in Beth's shoulders eased.

"Good luck. Have fun. Be safe. Let me know how it goes and I love you," Kate added.

"I love you, too. Both of you." Beth hung up the phone and threw on her clothes, scrunching her short hair a few times for effect. Then she grabbed her keys and raced out of the house. If she didn't hurry she'd be late.

It took her only five minutes to reach Griffin's neighborhood. The address was near hers and a little more than a mile from Little Ray. It was one of the row houses that had been built during the eighteen hundreds for Belmont's dockworkers. A developer had bought and renovated the houses as part of a revitalization project for year-round Belmont residents. Beth's father and brother had worked on the project before the recession wiped out the town's construction industry.

She scanned the houses for his number. When she found it, she carefully maneuvered Martha into a narrow parking spot on the street.

She got out of the van, picked up her purse and another bag, and slammed the door shut. Then she squared her shoulders and bounded up Griffin's front steps two at a time. When she reached the front door, she raised her hand and knocked softly.

Her heart hammered in her chest and she forced herself to take a few deep breaths. *You've got this.*

The thud of footsteps sounded on the other side before the door swung open.

She swallowed hard. In front of her stood Griffin, his shaggy, blond hair falling into his green eyes. He wore low-slung jeans, a pair of scuffed work boots, and a form-fitting plaid button-down. He stood with one hand leaning against the door frame, as his eyes raked over her.

Then his mouth curved into a smile. "Thanks for coming. You look great."

Goose bumps broke out over her skin and her face heated. He looked more than great.

He stared at her another long moment before he stepped forward and wrapped an arm around her. She rose onto her tiptoes and returned the hug. The warmth of his body enveloped her as his coffee scent filled her nose.

She momentarily lost herself in the rise and fall of his chest. Then plastered a bright smile on her face and took a step back.

She was here for dinner, not to melt into a puddle on his doorstep.

"Come on in." He held the door and she stepped through. On the right was a staircase to the second floor. On the left was a cozy living room, with an overstuffed sofa and matching arm chair. Straight ahead was a kitchen, with gleaming stainless steel surfaces and slate tile floors.

She pulled a bottle from the bag and placed it in Griffin's hand. "Coffee liqueur. I made it for you."

"You made it?" The corners of his mouth lifted. "Of course you did."

His eyes fixed on her face and her pulse pounded in her ears. She licked her lips nervously and his gaze traveled to her mouth, where it stayed.

After a long beat he gestured to the kitchen. "Dinner's ready. I hope you don't mind eating in the kitchen. I never use the dining room. It's too big and formal."

The kitchen was bathed in candlelight and a vase with white flowers sat in the middle of the table, surrounded by cardboard take-out containers. She grinned as she recognized the logos. Thai Number One. The best food in Belmont and possibly on the entire face of the planet.

She closed her eyes and inhaled the aroma of lemongrass.

When she opened her eyes again, he stood in front of a chair, which he'd pulled from the table.

Her heart fluttered. With shaky legs she crossed the room and sat.

Her eyes flickered to the chair next to her, where a large, red plastic booster seat perched. She gestured with her thumb. "Let me guess. That one's for you?"

He chuckled as he pulled a bottle of wine from the refrigerator and popped the cork. "You got me. I'm too short for the table. Plus I make a mess when I eat."

She raised her eyebrows. "No wonder you asked me for dinner at your house. This way nobody can see your horrible table manners."

He chuckled. "Yes. Absolutely." His eyes turned soft as he poured wine into her glass. "But really, thanks for coming over. I know it might seem weird for a first date, but with Mabel…" He waved a hand toward the stairs as he trailed off.

Her heart skittered. A date. He'd said it aloud, which made it officially official.

She shrugged and took a sip of the wine, trying to cover the goofy grin that threatened to stretch across her face. "You offered to feed me. I don't say no to food."

His eyes danced as he settled into the chair across from her. "Not just any food. Thai Number One, the best food in Belmont. Possibly the entire planet."

She grinned at him. He had good taste.

"The planet, huh? Is that why you moved to Belmont?"

In the summer the town was a resort for tourists. Some people came to relax on the beach, while others came for the sailing, volleyball tournaments, and surfing competitions. Not to mention the seafood. The crabs were to die for, a fact she and Kate had used as a pickup line on tourist boys when they were in high school.

But most of the year-round residents could trace their families back generations. Like her. Until a few years earlier, not a single Beverly had ever lived outside of Belmont for longer than the four years it took to complete college. That was before her brother moved away, followed by her parents. No matter what they said, they could never convince her that Florida had the same cozy charm as Belmont. All beaches were not made alike.

He handed her a container and she spooned rice noodles onto her plate. Her mouth watered as the steam curled into the air.

His smile dropped as he focused his attention on a container of curry. "It's as good a reason as any."

A long pause stretched between them. Why had he moved to Belmont? Family? Friends? Surely he hadn't bought Little Ray and moved his daughter to a brand-new town on a whim.

She bit her lip. "Where are you from? Before this?"

He twirled a forkful of noodles on his plate. "Shepherdsville, Ohio."

She rested her fork against the side of her plate. Clearly if she wanted some biographical details she was going to have to work for them. Maybe Kate was right. Maybe he was like the mysterious Mr. Rochester.

Then he smiled and warmth spread through her. He was complex, maybe, but definitely not broody. Not at all like Mr. Rochester.

She took a bite of curry, the spicy tang caressing her tongue. "Tell me about Shepherdsville."

His forehead furrowed. "It's the most boring, land-locked Midwestern town you could possibly imagine. Other than cows and corn, there's nothing there. Nothing exciting ever happens there."

Then he winked at her. "Tell me about Belmont. Your Belmont."

She took another sip of wine and leaned forward to rest her elbows on the table. "My Belmont? It's probably not any different from your Belmont."

He covered her hand with his, the warmth of his fingers seeping into her skin. "I highly doubt that. You're a lot more interesting than me. Besides, you've lived here your whole life?"

She found herself nodding. "Yup. Born and raised. I went through all the local Belmont schools, then Belmont College for the Arts. All my friends are here."

She paused and swallowed hard. She'd been about to say all her family lived here, too, but that wasn't true anymore.

He laced his fingers through hers and squeezed. "You're braver than me."

She burst into surprised laughter. "Brave? I've spent my entire life in a town of sixty thousand people."

She'd never really gone anywhere or done anything. Once upon a time she'd imagined herself as a local business owner who would help the community of Belmont grow. When that dream went up in smoke, she'd reassured herself that something great was right around the corner. Now, two years later, she was starting to wish it would hurry up.

He released her hand and speared another forkful of noodles. "You're brave, even if you don't admit it."

Her face flushed.

He watched her openly now, a smile playing on the corners of his lips. "You know exactly who you are, and you don't pretend, even for a second, to be anybody else. Do you know how unusual that is?"

Her throat grew thick. Did she know exactly who she was? Could have fooled her.

She dropped her eyes to her plate. "I don't think anybody knows who they are exactly. At least not all the time. Sometimes I feel like I'm a different person every day. Every hour and every minute, even."

His eyes turned thoughtful and he nodded. "Point taken, although I think you also just proved mine. Not many people realize they're constantly changing, constantly evolving. In that way we're like the best musicians. Take the Beatles. They started with *Please Please Me*, and they were working with a new sound which was revolutionary in its own way. People went nuts over it. Then they started to branch out and experiment and four years letter you had *Sgt. Pepper's Lonely Heart Club Band*."

As he spoke he gestured animatedly with his hands.

Her breath caught. Without even trying she'd just unlocked another Griffin mystery.

"You love music."

He paused to smile at her. "Hell yes. Doesn't everyone?"

She laughed. "I hope so. But you really love music. You're passionate about music."

He nodded slowly. "I am. I'm passionate about music. And you're passionate about..."

He raised his eyebrows at her.

She swallowed. "Um, everything? Muffins and baking and art and gardening and sewing and creating and teaching kids." She shrugged.

"What did you study at BCA?"

She sighed. That was another long story. "When I started I was in the illustration program. But then I became friends with this girl who was into metalworking, so I started hanging out at her studio and eventually I became obsessed with the idea of glassblowing." Her face heated. "Like I said, I change my mind a lot."

"You say that like it's a bad thing." He reached for her hand and squeezed. "Trust me. I've changed a few times myself. Anyone who says they haven't is lying."

"Daddy!" A wail sounded from upstairs.

Across from her Griffin froze, then shoved his chair back from the table.

"She probably just wants a glass of water. I'll be back in a few minutes."

She gave him a reassuring smile. "Don't worry about it. I'm fine."

She eyed the cardboard containers. Would it be wrong to sneak a little more food? The pad thai was especially good tonight.

He smiled and nodded at the containers. "Please kill off the noodles while I'm gone, so I don't have to. And save room for chocolate."

Her pulse fluttered. A sexy man who encouraged her to eat copious amounts of Thai food and fed her chocolate? Jackpot.

* * *

Griffin pulled the bedroom door shut behind him and glanced at his watch. Nine fifteen. It had taken him a full thirty minutes to get Mabel back to sleep.

His gut tightened. What was Beth doing? Was she bored? Annoyed? How the hell did single parents date?

He sighed heavily and headed down the stairs. Hopefully she wasn't too irritated. He was a dad first and foremost. Beth knew that.

When he reached the first-floor hallway, the sight of her stopped him in his path. Beth sat on the sofa, a book in her lap, her legs curled underneath her. As if sensing his gaze, she glanced up at him and smiled. Her eyes sparkled.

His breath caught and a flame ignited inside of him.

"Is she okay? I can go if we're keeping her up." Her voice was barely louder than a whisper.

"No." The word practically jumped from his mouth. He clenched his fist at his side. "Don't go. Stay. She's normally a heavy sleeper."

Otherwise he would never have invited Beth over.

She gave a small nod. "If you're not worried about it, I'd love to stay."

The muscles in his shoulders relaxed. "Good. You want to try the coffee liqueur? I have some chocolates to go with it."

He'd stopped by a local chocolate shop on his way to pick up Mabel. If they were good, he was going to start stocking them at Little Ray.

She set the book on the coffee table and grinned at him. "I'm game if you are."

"I'll be right back." He ducked into the kitchen and grabbed two tumblers, the box of bittersweet-chocolate truffles, and the bottle of amber liquid. As he turned, the empty table grabbed his attention.

She'd cleaned up. The containers, the dishes, the wineglasses, everything. She'd put them all away. When was the last time he'd had someone to help with dishes?

The back of his neck prickled. He paused, struggling to identify the emotion. Was it hope? Expectation? Anticipation? Or a combination of all three?

Whatever it was, he kind of liked it.

He shook his head, willing himself back to the present. This wasn't the time to start psychoanalyzing himself. Beth was waiting for him.

When he returned to the living room, he eased himself into the cushions beside her on the sofa and poured two glasses. She reached for hers and held it in the air, her forehead wrinkled in concentration.

"To coffee and muffins," she finally said.

"To coffee and muffins."

They clinked their glasses, but before he could take a sip, he found himself mesmerized by her soft, pink lips.

She raised the tumbler and took a small swallow, then erupted in sputtering coughs.

"Are you okay?" She hunched forward, and he pressed his palm on the center of her back, rubbing in circles.

Slowly the redness of her face faded and her coughs slowed. "Man, that's strong. I think I accidentally made moonshine."

Curious, he lifted his own glass to his lips and took the tiniest of tastes. Liquid fire burned a path down his throat. He held his breath in a desperate attempt to avoid coughing.

Pretend you like it. Don't hurt her feelings.

Beth burst into giggles. "I swear I followed the recipe I found online exactly."

He eyed the bottle. "Are you sure you searched 'how to make liqueur' and not 'how to make a bomb' or 'how to poison your date'?"

Her giggles grew until tears ran down her cheeks. "Maybe we could cut it with something? Milk? Water?…Lighter fluid?"

He lost it, laughing so hard his sides hurt. When he collected himself, she was looking at him wide-eyed.

Adrenaline pounded. It had been so long since he'd laughed like that, especially with another adult, over a joke that was meant for adults. He felt lighter, freer than he had in years.

He leaned forward and slid his hand along her jawline to cup her cheek. There was a slight pressure as she leaned into his touch. Her lips parted almost imperceptibly as she tilted her chin upward.

He covered the space between them slowly, inching closer with every ragged breath. His pulse pounded as his lips met hers, brushing against their silky softness. His hand slid to the back of her neck, urging her closer as his tongue flicked into her mouth.

She let out a small moan and her hands rose to twine in his hair. He lost himself in the kiss, his tongue stroking hers as she molded herself to him.

There was a creak from the second floor and she jumped back. Her gaze flew to the top of the stairs. "Is that Mabel?"

He tugged her back into his lap. "No. It's just an old house.

Mabel really is a heavy sleeper. Plus she likes to have a piggy-back when she gets out of bed."

As much as he'd wanted to see Beth, he'd never have risked having Mabel find her in the living room. There was zero chance she'd get out of bed and come downstairs on her own.

The corners of Beth's mouth lifted, but her gaze strayed back to the stairs.

"Trust me. When Mabel walks on these old wooden floors she sounds like a herd of water buffalo. We'd have plenty of time to hide you in a closet before she made it down here."

She giggled, then relaxed into him. He pulled her closer, until her head came to rest on his chest. They sat side by side, comfortably snuggled together.

"Do you want another glass of wine? Or a beer?" He should probably find something else to occupy his hands and his mouth. The kiss had been incredible and he wanted more, but he couldn't let himself move too fast. Already he could tell that things with Beth had the potential to be…something.

"Nah, I'm good. I have to drive and that sip of coffee liqueur probably put me over the limit."

He laughed as she nestled into him.

"What made you decide to move to Belmont?" she asked.

He tensed.

It's a perfectly normal question. He could answer truthfully without going into the whole custody battle. As little experience as he'd had these last few years, even he knew that was too heavy for a first date.

"I was in a band. We toured for a lot and we'd come through Belmont a few times. You know how somewhere can stick in your mind? It's not necessarily the place, it's the combination of the place and the time, but it develops this warm, fuzzy, idyllic quality in your head?"

She gave a small murmur, a sound of agreement.

"Belmont took on that quality for me. I always thought in a vague way that I would retire here when my music career was over. But then Mabel came along and I wound up quitting the band without a plan in place. It was easiest just to move home for a while."

He swallowed hard. This is where the truth got tricky. "I spent time online looking at properties in Belmont and one day I came across a restaurant listed for sale at a really good price, so I bought it."

His palms began to sweat. She didn't need to know that he'd been stuck in Shepherdsville for eighteen months while the custody case was pending. Or that he'd bought Little Ray the day he won custody, when he was desperate to get the hell out of his hometown. That was a conversation for another time.

She pushed back from his chest to examine his face, a smile playing on her lips. "You were in a band?"

He chuckled. He'd forgotten how that one little phrase could affect women.

He lifted a hand to her hair, brushing his knuckles over the soft curls. "I was."

"What kind of band?"

His blood pounded. God, he wanted to kiss her again.

"Rock. Hard rock with some metal mixed in."

She raised an eyebrow. "Interesting. Did you always know you wanted to be a musician?"

"I learned how to play the guitar when I was five and then in middle school I got my hands on some Metallica CDs and became obsessed with Cliff Burton. I taught myself how to play the bass."

He'd watched MTV and VH1 obsessively, his attention focused on the finger work of the bass players. He'd copied them until it clicked. By his junior year of high school he'd been writing his own riffs.

"A friend of mine formed the band when we were in high school. Eventually we got pretty popular and I dropped out of college, the rest is Thorny Lemon history."

Her eyes went wide. "You were in Thorny Lemon? Are you kidding me?"

His spine tingled. She knew who they were? Beth didn't strike him as their usual type of fan.

She thwacked his chest. "I saw you guys! When you were in Belmont! My brother freaking loved you."

His mouth went dry. She'd seen them live?

He and his bandmates had actively cultivated the typical rock and roll reputation, playing along with the perception that they were hard partiers and womanizers. The reality was far from the truth, but Angela's parents had still been able to use it against him in the custody case.

His gut clenched. Was that what Beth would think of him, too?

She snuggled into his side. "That's crazy. So you weren't just being nice when you said you've changed a few times, too."

The tightness in his gut eased. He should have guessed Beth

wouldn't judge him on appearances. After all, she dressed like a bumblebee for work.

A damn sexy bumblebee.

He swallowed hard. *Focus.*

"Nope, I was completely serious. So, does he live around here? Your brother?" He was tired of talking about himself and his past.

She sighed loudly. "I wish. The recession hit the construction industry in Belmont hard. My brother moved to Florida for a job. My parents hung on longer, thinking the economy would turn around, but they joined him almost two years ago."

"I'm sorry." That had to be hard. As much as he missed his own family, at least it had been his choice to leave.

She sighed. "It sucks. But he'll be excited when I tell him I know Griffin Hall. You're a real rock star!"

The muscles in his neck bunched and tensed. That wasn't how he wanted her to think of him.

She glanced up at him, her dark eyes studying his expression. "Sorry. Is that weird for you?"

He smiled hesitantly. "Yeah. Kind of."

"Then let's not talk about it anymore." She wrinkled her nose before she leaned up and brushed her lips over his.

His chest swelled. Could she be more perfect?

She nestled back against him and they lapsed into comfortable silence. Only the sound of their mingled breaths hung in the air.

After a few moments, Beth let out a loud yawn and clapped a hand over her mouth. "I'm sorry. I have the internal clock of an octogenarian."

He swallowed the yawn that was building in his throat. It was late for him, too. Where had the night gone?

He stroked a hand over her hair. "No problem. I'm the exact same way. I have to be up before the coffee-drinking masses."

She sighed loudly as she sat up and stretched her arms over her head. "Then I should probably let you go to sleep."

Suddenly his chest felt naked without her curled against him. "Right. Yes. We should both get some sleep." He swallowed hard and forced himself to stand, then extended his hand to her.

She folded her fingers into his, and he gently tugged her to her feet. They stood face-to-face, mere inches apart.

She smiled at him as she wrapped her fingers around his jaw and kissed him firmly on the mouth. The soft velvet of her tongue sent shock waves through his body.

It took all his willpower to release her when the kiss ended. They stood for a moment, staring at each other.

In the old days, before Mabel, he would have asked her to stay. He would have kissed her until she was breathless and teased her with his touch. But his daughter was asleep upstairs. He couldn't be that guy anymore.

Beth gestured toward the door. "I'm going to make myself leave now and I'll see you soon."

He nodded. "Text me when you get home. So I know you got there okay."

The smile she gave him was blinding. Then she turned and let herself through the door.

He slumped against the door frame, watching her figure disappear into the darkness. He couldn't wait to see her again.

CHAPTER SIX

Griffin sat in his windowless, cinder block office, typing on his laptop. He glanced at the closed door again and tapped his feet impatiently underneath his desk. Beth would be here any minute.

His attention wandered to his phone and their texts from that morning, which were still open on his computer screen.

> Beth: I had a big special order for the weekend and wound up with about two dozen extra muffins. You want me to come by Little Ray and drop them off? Say two o'clock?

Griffin: Yes. Even though I know you're just making up an excuse to see me.

She'd sent an emoticon of a face sticking its tongue out.

> Beth: I thought you'd be happy to have the muffins, but if you don't want them...

Griffin: Oh, I want them. You know I want them. I just thought

kissing you was its own reward. Who knew there were
added perks?

Beth: Well, now that you mention it, the cost of a muffin just
went up. One kiss per muffin.

He grinned even now, rereading it.

Griffin: How many do you have? Twenty-four? I'll take
another hundred then.

He sighed as he settled back into the office chair and forced his
attention back to the email he was drafting to the dry-goods
provider.

It contained only two words—"Please send"—followed by
a semicolon. He'd been sitting here for twenty minutes, and
all he'd managed to think about was Beth. The warmth of her
brown eyes, the curve of her hips, the way her shirt rode up
and gave him a glimpse of her stomach when she stretched her
arms over her head.

He gripped the notebook in his lap and forced himself to
stare at the numbers. A thousand of the biodegradable coffee
cups. Two thousand wooden coffee stirrers. Three thousand
paper napkins, with the Little Ray logo.

Outside his office door he heard voices and the clunk of
boxes being set on the metal prep tables. It was her. Beth was
here.

He pushed his chair back from the desk. One of the wheels
was broken and it rolled unevenly across the floor until it
bumped into a filing cabinet.

He strode across the room and jerked the door open. The
sight of her curly hair made his heart rate speed.

"Hey."

She turned to face him, a smile spreading wide across her face. "Hey to you, too."

Next to her his employee Brian was already placing the muffins on trays. "Hey, boss, you want me to put them all out now or save some until tomorrow?"

"Just put them all out now. First come, first served." He'd already put out a blast on Facebook and Twitter announcing their arrival.

He raised an eyebrow at Beth. "Could I see you in my office for a minute, please?"

"Sure, we should talk about next Tuesday's order." She spoke loudly enough for Brian to overhear and winked at Griffin.

He quashed the chuckle that built inside of him. They hadn't talked about how they would treat each other at work, but discretion was important to him. He didn't need his employees to know all of his personal business.

Leave it to Beth to intuit that. And to dance right up the line.

He showed her into his office and closed the door behind them. As soon as it clicked shut, he turned around, swept her into his arms and kissed her hard.

She giggled. "Is this like the principal's office of Little Ray? Am I in trouble?"

He wrapped an arm around her waist, pulling her closer, and lowered his mouth to hers again.

She tasted sweet, like honey, and her body softened into his as she increased the pressure of their lips.

He felt himself harden, but he didn't pull away. Instead he slipped his tongue into her mouth, eager to taste all of her.

She arched against him and tilted her head, opening herself to him fully. He shifted, so his hardness was cradled by the soft curve of her belly.

He broke the kiss to rest his forehead on hers as he breathed raggedly. "You're definitely not in trouble. How many muffins did you bring? Two dozen? I owe you and I just assumed you were here to collect on the debt."

Her laughter rang through the cramped office. "Is this a trick? To get me to bring more muffins? I told you, I'm a one-woman show. I can only bake so much."

He tightened his grip on her hip. "Maybe you upped the cost of your muffins retroactively. Maybe I'm making up for a full month of muffin deliveries."

She nodded. "That's definitely it. You owe me. And I'm the most intimidating loan shark you've ever met. I have my ways of collecting."

She grabbed the front of his shirt and pulled him back to her, rising on her toes to press her lips against his. His pulse pounded in his ears and he wrapped his arms around her waist, losing himself in the kiss.

A knock sounded on the door. He cursed and released her.

"Yes?"

"We have a huge line and Cora went on break. I need help at the register for ten minutes until she comes back." Brian's muffled voice came through the door.

"Okay. I'll be right there," he yelled.

Then he turned to Beth and frowned. "Sorry. We're short-staffed."

He reached for her hand and pulled her closer. "When can I see you again?"

She rested her cheek against his chest, her breath warm through the fabric of his shirt. "My schedule's pretty flexible. You're the one with the business and the kid."

His stomach clenched. *Mabel.*

What was it about Beth that made him forget his responsibilities? That his decisions weren't just his anymore? Everything he did had the potential to affect Mabel.

She'd already had her life tossed upside down once. He wouldn't do that to her again. Which was why he needed to take this slower. He had to be more cautious.

He swallowed the lump in his throat. "What time do you normally finish deliveries for the day? Does lunchtime work for you?"

He'd take her out. On a real date. In public. Where they could sit and talk and he'd resist the urge to see and taste every inch of her.

"Lunch works." Her cheery voice snapped him from his reverie. *Concentrate.*

"Monday? At noon?"

There was another knock at the door. She stepped away from him and he quickly crossed the room.

"Yes?" He opened it a crack.

Brian's face was pale on the other side. "The computer is acting up again. I've tried to run this guy's card three times and it keeps crashing."

His jaw clenched. Stupid computer. This was what he got for hiding in his office, making out with Beth instead of running his damn business. At the moment, he was doing a shitty job of balancing personal and professional. No wonder he hadn't been on a date since he'd opened Little Ray.

He felt a slight pressure, as Beth pressed her palms against his back. "Go. Save the day for the coffee drinkers of Belmont. And text me about Monday."

He paused only long enough to fix her with a grin. "Until Monday."

Then he followed Brian through the partition to the front of the coffee house. Right now it was time to work.

* * *

Beth slipped off her shoes and dug her toes into the sand. The salty breeze ruffled her hair as she scanned the parking lot. Griffin had told her to meet him here at noon. So where was he?

"Beth!" The voice came from behind her.

She turned toward the water and spotted him, in a T-shirt and board shorts, waving his arms in the air.

She couldn't help it. A grin spread across her face and she found herself rushing across the sand to him.

She came to a stop when she reached him, pausing to process the soft, blue blanket on the sand, the silverware and plates and champagne glasses.

Her heart raced, as she lifted her gaze to him. "You made a picnic!"

Then she threw her arms around his neck and planted a kiss on his mouth. "I love picnics!"

He chuckled and trailed his knuckles across her cheek. "I had a feeling you would, but Sarah confirmed it."

She closed her eyes and let Griffin's coffee-caramel scent mix with the sea air. She nuzzled into his neck and inhaled deeply, burning the moment into her memory.

He planted a soft kiss on her temple. "Are you hungry?"

With a sigh she released him. "Yes, starving. What's for lunch?"

She lowered herself onto the blanket, in front of one of the place settings. Griffin settled himself across from her, then reached for a bottle of sparkling water and poured it into her champagne glass.

"The other night you said you'd been born here and raised here, and you went to BCA. I didn't know if you'd gotten to travel much."

Her lungs constricted. She hadn't traveled much. Especially not compared to someone like him, a rock star who had spent years touring Asia and South America and Europe. She was a townie, a term that made her cringe.

He lifted a few containers out of a picnic basket and opened them on the blanket. "But you remind me of this town in Italy. I know that seems like a weird thing to say, that you remind me of a town. But it's full of all these paths that take you to completely unexpected places. Everywhere you turn, someone is trying to feed you. Everyone smiles all the time, and they have a little street theater with puppets that the kids gather around to watch."

He lifted his eyes to her and grinned. "If you were a place, Beth, you would be this place. We played a concert in a city nearby, but we had a day off and I explored the town by myself.

The whole time I kept thinking how great it would be to share it with someone. The other night it came to me: I had to have lunch with you in Urbino."

Her breath caught. Wow.

He gestured to the food he'd laid out on the blanket. Olives, figs, cheese, bread, dried fruit. Her mouth watered just looking at it.

"So here you go. Lunch in Urbino."

Her eyes stung and she blinked hard. This could not be happening. This could not be real.

"Wow."

The corners of his mouth dropped and his eyebrows furrowed. "Do you like it?" He dropped his gaze to his lap, where his hands fidgeted. "Is it too much?"

She threw herself at him, covering his face with kisses, not caring if she knocked anything over. "It's the most incredible thing anyone has ever done for me."

His fingers closed around her waist and he tugged her into his lap. He pressed his mouth to hers and used the tip of his tongue to trace the seam of her lips.

A high-pitched whistle pierced the air. She raised her head and found a group of teenage boys giving them the thumbs-up.

Her face heated and she crawled back to her spot on the other side of the blanket.

She reached for the container of olives and spooned a few onto her plate. "I feel like I should warn you that dessert is entirely off-theme."

He raised an eyebrow and popped a fig into his mouth. "Oh yeah?"

She nodded. "Oh yeah."

Then she reached for the plastic bag in her purse and plopped it onto the blanket, so that one of the cookies was faceup inside the package.

He leaned toward it, his eyes narrowing. "What kind of cookie is that?"

She'd iced them pink and then used magenta piping to create little curlicues. "Pig butt."

His gaze jerked to hers and he blinked a few times. "A pig-butt cookie?"

The tickle in her throat became too much, she burst into giggles. "Just the decoration, not the flavoring. I found them on Pinterest. Nailed it, right?"

He threw his head back and laughed. "Yup. You nailed it. That is most definitely a pig's ass. Martha Stewart, the person not the van, would be impressed."

With a giggle, she tipped her head back to let the sunshine warm her face.

It was as near to perfect as a date could be.

CHAPTER SEVEN

Later that night, Beth stood backstage behind the curtains, frantically digging through one of the costume boxes. Where had Addie's princess crown gone? She never went anywhere without it. Had one of the other kids accidentally taken it home?

Addie brought the crown to class every week, regardless of the story they were acting out. When they'd performed the Pied Piper, Addie had worn the crown on top of her brown felt rat head.

Beth leaned forward and parted the red velvet curtains to peek at the stage. The last of the kids were trickling out the door with their parents. Addie and Mabel chased each other through the theater seats, while Griffin stood on the stage staring at his phone.

Her heart leaped. He'd arrived over twenty minutes ago and he was still here. Was he waiting for her? Waiting until all the other kids went home, so they could have a moment together?

They'd already agreed to play it cool in front of Mabel, but that didn't mean they couldn't talk.

Her pulse sped and she bent to rifle through the box of fabric one more time. How had she let Addie lose her crown? She'd been in a fog the last three days, ever since her make-out session with Griffin in his office. Her skin heated at the memory.

She rocked back on her heels and stared at the fabric strewn around her. This was a disaster. She'd just have to tell Addie's mom, Gwen, that she'd lost the crown. Maybe a night of free babysitting would help lessen the sting.

She heard the sharp clip of high heels on the stage floor and watched as Gwen, in a gray suit with her brown hair twisted into a chignon, approached Griffin.

Gwen had the princess crown clasped firmly in her hand. *Oh, thank God.* Beth flopped into a cross-legged position. Addie must have left it at home today. How had she missed that? She really was in a fog.

With a shake of her head, she stuffed a few dresses into the costume box. She needed to pay more attention. This was her job and the kids deserved all of her energy.

Onstage, Gwen held out her hand to Griffin. "Are you Mabel's dad?"

Beth peered from behind the curtain and allowed her gaze to travel over him. She started at the worn work boots on his feet, up to the slim-cut, dark jeans, over the fitted flannel, up to the stubble on his chin, and to his bright, green eyes. Her stomach did a flip. Who could blame her for losing focus? He was gorgeous.

Griffin lifted his eyes from his phone and shook Gwen's hand. "I am. Griffin Hall. And you are?"

"Gwen Maloney. Addie's mom."

He gave a nod. "Nice to meet you. Mabel talks about Addie all the time."

Gwen smiled. "Yes, they've gotten close. We should set up a playdate sometime." Her gaze flicked to the children. "In fact, we have a group of single parents who get together every other week or so. The kids play together and we talk. You know, spend some time with other adults."

His eyebrows furrowed. "Sounds interesting. But I have kind of a hectic work schedule."

"Oh, believe me, we all know how that can be. Which is why it's so important to get out and spend time with other single parents. You know, other adults who understand what it's like. And we take turns watching each other's children when someone needs a night out. I even met my boyfriend there." Gwen's tone was warm and encouraging.

The corners of Griffin's mouth lifted. "All right. That could be good. My email's in the preschool directory. Let me know when your meetings are and I'll try to make it."

Her stomach hollowed out, and she quickly chided herself. It was good for Griffin to spend time with people. Especially people who knew how tough it could be as a single parent. Unlike her.

Her throat grew tight and she had to work to swallow. So far they'd managed to shove the parenting thing onto the back burner, but they couldn't keep it there forever. And she really liked him. Which meant...she froze. What the hell did it mean? Would she ever be able to understand Griffin's life the way someone like Gwen did? How would Mabel react when she found out they were dating? What would her role be when it came to Mabel?

Don't get ahead of yourself. It was the advice she would have given one of her friends in the exact same situation. They were having fun. He was hot and she liked spending time with him. Why worry about labels and the future and all that crazy shit?

A lump formed in her throat. She swallowed hard, shoved the rest of the costumes into the trunk, and quietly snapped it shut. This was silly. She was being silly. Everyone had complications in their lives. You either made it work or you didn't. For her and Griffin, it was too soon to tell which category they'd fall into.

She stood, brushed off her jeans, lifted the trunk, and carried it back to its place in the corner. Then she walked back onstage.

She scanned the theater. Gwen and Addie were gone. On the stage Griffin paced, his phone pressed to his ear. Mabel sat on the stage stairs, her jacket and backpack on.

Beth approached her. "Hey, Mabel! You all packed up and ready to go?"

Mabel leaped from her spot and wrapped her arms around Beth's waist. "Yup! Daddy said we can make grilled cheese for dinner and then before I take my bath, we can go get ice cream!"

Funny. That was her idea of a perfect night, too. "Where do you like to get ice cream?"

Mabel let go of her waist and frowned, tiny wrinkles lining

her forehead. "The place. With the cow on the front. And the writing is green. And the chairs are yellow. And if you ask nicely they'll put some of the ice cream on a little spoon so you can try a new one, but I always get the bubblegum."

She grinned. D'Amico's. With the ice cream scooper who, according to Kate, wished he was really a stripper. Mabel was right. Bubblegum was the best flavor.

Griffin crossed the stage to join them, a frown on his face. He rested a hand on Mabel's head. "Sorry, kiddo, but we have to change our plans. Daddy has to go to work. We can do our special dinner tomorrow night."

Mabel's face fell and her chin began to wobble. "That's what you said last night." She stamped a tiny foot on the stage.

Griffin glanced at her, his eyebrows clearly knit with worry. "I know, honey and I'm really sorry. We're short-staffed again."

"I can babysit her." The words were out of her mouth before she could think. She babysat lots of kids who were in her class.

Griffin's gaze shot to her. "I can't ask you to do that."

She bit her lip. Mabel had heard, which meant she'd backed them both into a corner.

She caught his eyes and hoped he could somehow pick up on her thoughts. *I'd have offered even if I didn't spend all my time daydreaming about your naked body.*

Yeah. She definitely couldn't say that in front of his kid.

Mabel gripped her hand and stared up at her dad. "Please. Oh, please, Daddy. I don't want to go to work tonight. I want to stay with Beth."

A muscle in his jaw ticked.

"Griffin. It's just babysitting," she said softly.

He scraped a hand over his face. "Are you sure?" His voice was strained.

She ruffled a hand over Mabel's head. "Of course I'm sure. Mabel told me there's grilled cheese and ice cream."

He smiled tightly, then nodded. "Okay. Yes. Thank you. Mabel would love that."

Mabel squealed and jumped in the air.

"Mabel, would you please wait by the door so I can talk to Beth for a minute? I want to make sure she knows all the rules for babysitters."

"Okay!" Her feet echoed through the theater as she sprinted away from them.

Griffin's gaze pierced her and her heart raced. "You don't have to do this."

She shrugged, her stomach lurching. "It's just babysitting, I swear. I watch lots of the kids from the theater. It doesn't have anything to do with…" The words caught in her throat and she waved her hand between them.

He stepped forward. "You and me?" His eyes held hers. "It doesn't have anything to do with you and me?"

She swallowed hard. Right. Exactly. Nothing to do with them.

She lifted her chin. "Exactly."

They'd already agreed to keep their work and personal lives separate. Technically babysitting was work.

He cocked his head to one side, watching her. "So that means you'll let me pay you?"

"Not in money." Her face heated as she realized the implication. A lazy grin overtook his face and she coughed, trying not to choke on her embarrassment.

"What I meant is, I'd accept payment in the form of coffee. And maybe a few gluten-free, maple-bacon donuts." Kate loved those suckers.

She took a deep breath and raised an eyebrow at him.

His eyes danced with amusement as he held out his hand. "Babysitting for coffee. Agreed. Now let's get her car seat into Martha."

She shook his hand. It was a deal. A business deal.

They could totally pull this off. She could babysit Mabel. She could date Griffin. And the two things wouldn't get muddled together. She'd make sure of it.

* * *

Griffin gritted his teeth as he stalked up the sidewalk to Little Ray. The credit card machine had gone down, again. A frustrated customer had yelled at Cora, who'd dissolved into tears.

All of which was bad enough. But then he'd disappointed Mabel, and in front of Beth.

His gut twisted. He owed her a debt he wasn't entirely sure he could repay. They could joke about payment in the form of coffee and kisses and muffins, but being there for Mabel was invaluable. What Beth had done for his daughter tonight? He could never put a price on that.

He reached the front door and yanked it open, the bell tinkling as he stepped inside. Sarah stood behind the counter, her apron dotted with coffee and crumbs.

She threw her hands in the air. "Praise Jesus, hallelujah, the cavalry has arrived."

He narrowed his eyes at her and scanned the coffee shop.

There were only a few guests. Thunder. Ralph. The lady whose sweater was always covered in cat fur. At least only the regulars had heard her theatrics.

"Where's Cora?"

She jerked a thumb toward the back. "I put her in your office. By now it's probably flooded with tears. Be careful. You might want to bring a pair of water wings."

He shook his head and headed for the back. Much as he wanted to strangle her right now, it would only exacerbate his staffing problem.

He knocked on the door to his office. "Cora?"

When she didn't respond, he cracked the door and peered inside. She was passed out in his broken chair, collapsed onto his desk with her head resting on her folded arms. Loud snores punctuated the air.

He sighed and slumped against the wall. She was just tired. Like the rest of them. He really needed to hire some more staff.

He trudged back to the front counter.

"So?" Sarah slid over to make room for him.

"So what?" He pulled out his phone and looked up the number for the computer company.

"Where's my little buddy?" She glanced through the restaurant, as if he'd hidden Mabel under one of the tables.

His throat tightened. "With Beth. Eating grilled cheese and getting ice cream."

Out of the corner of his eye, he saw Sarah's head swivel in his direction. "Well that's a development."

He shook his head vigorously. "Nope. It is most certainly

not a development. I told May I had to come back to work, she had a meltdown and Beth took pity on us. She's babysitting."

Sarah poked him in the side. "Babysitting, eh? Is that what they call it?"

He clenched his jaw and hoped steam wouldn't come pouring out of his ears. He was crazy about Beth, but he'd just shown her all his inadequacies as a father. She'd taken pity on him, pure and simple. And if he was realistic about it, he had to admit that it might change the way he felt about her. When he pictured the joy on Mabel's face back at the theater, he was overcome by the urge to grab Beth and crush her to his chest. It made him want to hold on to her and not let go.

Which was the opposite of how he'd told himself it should be between them. He was supposed to be taking this slow and avoiding rash, impulsive decisions.

"I don't want to talk about it." Especially not with Sarah, who was Beth's friend, too. No, he'd have to figure this out in the privacy of his own head. "What I want to do is call the computer company and get this shit fixed once and for all."

He punched the little phone icon on his screen and held the phone to his ear, waiting as it rang.

It flipped over to voice mail. "Hi this is Chad with Computers for You."

With every word of the message, Griffin's blood pressure rose. By the time the recording finally beeped, he was ready to explode.

"This is Griffin Hall with Little Ray of Sunshine. Our computer crashed. Again. So I need you to come fix this freaking thing first thing in the morning."

He slammed the phone down on the counter, once again thankful for the military grade cell phone case he'd bought after Mabel threw his phone out a third-floor window in an attempt to make the Angry Birds fly farther.

He turned to Sarah. "You can handle this from here, right?"

She nodded mutely.

"Great. Then I'm going to go put my kid to bed."

He stalked back out the door. He could set things right with Cora tomorrow. Tonight, he just wanted to be a dad.

CHAPTER EIGHT

He lazily trailed a hand through her hair, his blood pounding as he drank in her image. She lay back on his sofa, a soft smile playing on her lips.

He'd made it back Monday night just in time to give Mabel her bath and put her to bed. But before Beth left, he'd made sure to invite her to lunch on Wednesday. This time, at his house.

Iron & Wine played in the background. He'd fallen in love with the soulful sound the first time he'd heard him, back when he was in his only year of college. In the last week the lyrics of "This Must Be the Place" had taken on a newfound resonance.

Beth slipped a hand under his shirt, and trailed her warm fingers over the skin of his chest. He sighed and closed his eyes, letting the flood of desire wash over him.

He'd made peace with the events of Monday night. If it changed Beth's opinion of him as a father, or if her relationship with his daughter changed the way he felt about her, then so be it. They'd cross that bridge when they got there.

For now, he just wanted to enjoy her.

He lowered his mouth to hers, his tongue entering and tasting the sweetness that was unique to Beth.

He trailed a kiss down her neck, to the hollow of her throat. Underneath him she shifted to align her body more perfectly with his. Her hand shook slightly and he grabbed it and raised it to his lips.

"Are you okay?"

Her pupils were dilated, her cheeks flushed.

"Mm-hmm." When she bit her lip like that every inch of him grew hard.

He kissed her neck again as his hand slid down the soft skin of her belly.

"We don't…If you…I know this must be hard for you."

He pulled his mouth from hers. "What?"

Was she okay? What on earth was she talking about?

"I know with, um, Mabel's mom and everything that happened, losing her, I don't know if you…" Her voice grew smaller and smaller until she trailed off completely.

Her throat worked as she swallowed. "I know it might be hard for you to be with someone else."

As soon as the words left her mouth, she snapped it shut. Her dark eyes watched him, waiting.

At first he almost laughed. But then the seriousness in her expression penetrated, making his chest ache. *Losing her?* What did Beth think had happened to Angela?

He scooped a hand under her neck, cradling it, and

looked into her eyes. "Nothing about you is hard, Beth. You're the softest, sweetest person I've ever met. Being with you is easy."

His throat burned, but he ignored it. Now wasn't the time to talk about Angela. In fact, right now he wanted to forget she'd ever existed.

"Okay." She gave a small nod.

He lifted her palm and pressed a kiss to it. How could he convince her? When it came to Beth Beverly there was nothing holding him back. That was the problem.

Her smile grew, like sunshine peeking through the clouds. She traced a finger along his jaw as her eyes locked with his, as if she could read the thoughts in his head.

Then, apparently satisfied with whatever she saw, she kissed him hard on the mouth and ran her palms under his shirt, along the skin of his chest. His skin sizzled and his restraint fractured. He was lost to the need to be bare, skin against skin, with her.

He fumbled, one handed, with the buttons of his shirt. After a few unsatisfying attempts he gave up and yanked it over his head, tossing it onto the ground beside them.

"Hold on." Beth flashed him a smile, then wiggled out from beneath him. His gut clenched as she stood from the sofa, staring down at him.

Where was she going? Why was she leaving?

Then she reached for the hem of her sundress, lifted it over her head, and dropped it unceremoniously to the floor.

His mouth salivated as his eyes raked over the compact curves of her body. His breaths were ragged and erratic, his eyes nearly aching with the attempt to burn the image into his memory.

She reached with a shaky hand to adjust the lace waistband of her polka-dotted underwear. He bolted into a sitting position, wrapped his large hands around the back of her thighs and pulled her to him. His tongue found the skin on her belly and he began to lick and nip at it.

Within seconds, Beth's legs were shaking. He pulled her down to straddle his lap.

"Griffin." The quaver in her voice stopped him short. Blood pounded in his ears.

She cupped his cheek with her hand. Then she smiled, illuminating all of the dark places inside of him.

"Do you have a condom?" Her voice was soft, which made his heart thud painfully in his chest.

He encircled her wrist and brought her palm to his mouth for a kiss. "Not yet."

He had too much to tell her and he sucked at talking about feelings. He had to show her.

* * *

Her eyes widened and she found herself staring at him. Not yet? What did that mean?

She was learning to accept that parts of Griffin's life were a mystery. Like Mabel's mom and her death, or the time he'd spent in Shepherdsville before he'd moved to Belmont.

The muscles in her abdomen tensed. If he wanted to keep certain things private, that was his business. But if he wanted to play with her, she didn't have time for that. She wasn't into games.

She broke eye contact and turned onto her side. She should go.

He slid his palm along her cheek and turned her head back to face him. "Beth. I want to make you feel good. Let me."

He ran a thumb over the hard peak of her nipple, sending shivers radiating down her body.

Need burned low inside of her. She lay back on the pillows, opening herself to him, embracing her exposure. Okay. She would let him.

A lazy grin curled his mouth. "That's much better."

He didn't kiss her for several minutes. Instead he used his mouth and his hands to explore her body. Every time she moaned or sighed he intensified his efforts, focusing on the area that had brought her pleasure.

He sucked one of her nipples into his mouth and flicked his tongue over the surface. Tension built between her legs, the desperation growing until it was all she could think about. She seized his hand and tentatively guided it between her folds.

He lowered his mouth to her ear. "Tell me how you want me to touch you."

Her face burned. She'd never exactly been good at that kind of thing. Role-playing, dirty talk, they were all talents that had escaped her.

She closed her eyes and focused on the sensation: the smooth warmth of his tongue on her hip bone, the gentle pressure of his thumb on her clitoris. When he slipped one finger inside her, something snapped and she cried out, arching her back upward.

He hoisted her hips farther onto the throw pillows and his strong hands spread her thighs apart.

"I have a condom in my purse." Her voice was breathless, nearly unrecognizable to her ears.

"Beth." He lowered his head between her legs and lifted his green eyes to meet hers. "I'm not doing that with you right now. Relax."

Her stomach twisted. "But what about you?"

He gave a low chuckle. "We'll get to that. Now stop distracting me."

He slipped one of his fingers inside her at the same time his tongue circled her clitoris.

She gasped, her muscles tightening around him. Griffin subtly increased the pressure of his tongue. Inside her, his finger curled as he brushed against her G spot.

Need built inside her, desire taking over her brain. She had to work to keep her hips still. Every featherlight touch of his tongue was perfect. She didn't want to ruin it and yet she needed more of him, all of him, deeper.

She groaned, half in frustration and half in pleasure. For a second he stopped, his tongue still.

Her blood pounded inside her head. *No don't stop! I need more!*

Then his tongue feathered over her clitoris again, his finger stroking inside her at exactly the right angle. Her breath caught and her hips jerked involuntarily. She curled her toes into the fabric of the sofa, her mind lost in a haze of bliss. Then she was coming, waves of satisfaction rolling over her, her body possessed by something too powerful to control.

When she finally finished and released a shuddering sigh he lifted himself to grin at her.

"You're very proud of yourself, aren't you?" she murmured.

"Maybe." He nibbled at her ear. "But I think I can do better."

Her heart pounded. Better? Was he insane? There was no way, in this universe, that better existed.

She held him tightly, running her hands over the hard muscles of his back, her cheek pressed against the warm skin of his chest.

"About that condom…" He wrapped one hand in her hair and leaned back to look at her. His skin glowed with a light sheen of perspiration.

Like a freaking sex god.

She giggled out loud. She must be drunk from her Griffin-induced orgasm.

"In my purse." She scrambled out from underneath him. So he'd blown her mind. She needed to get it together and focus, so she could blow his mind.

The double entendre made her giggle again. When she looked back at him, he was reclining on the sofa, watching her with a smile.

"Beth Beverly, I have no damn clue what you're laughing at, but I know you're sexy when you do."

She froze, naked in the middle of the hallway. She allowed her eyes to travel over his body: from his dirty-blond hair to his sage-green eyes to his firm shoulders, down the contours of his chest, to his waist, to…

Her breath caught and she gulped.

The most magnificent penis she'd ever seen. Another giggle rose inside of her, but she swallowed it down. This was absolutely not a laughing matter. Sex god had been a gross understatement.

His chest heaved and the head of his erect penis bobbed. She hastily jumped for her purse, tore through it, then triumphantly waved the condom as she flung herself on top of him.

"This is the part where you let me show you, yeah?" She ripped it open with her teeth. Technically a no-no according to her high school health teacher, but right now she didn't give a shit.

His eyes gleamed wickedly. "Fair's fair I guess."

He folded his hands behind his head, pretending to relax and let her take the reins.

Beth wrapped her fingers around his penis. His entire body jerked and he let out a low moan. His hands flew to grip her hips as she straddled his body.

"I guess I'm not in charge after all?" she whispered in his ear as she ran her tongue along the edge.

His fingers tightened around her hips. "Sorry. I can't help it."

She drew her palms down his chest, relishing the feel of his skin beneath her hands. The nape of her neck prickled in awareness. His eyes were glued to her, watching her every move.

Desire coursed through her blood, consuming all of her senses. She took the condom in her hands and unrolled it over the length of his penis. All the while he didn't move, didn't speak. He simply watched her, his eyes bright and penetrating, his muscles bunching with the strain of letting her take control.

When she was done, she braced her hands against his shoulders, leaned her forehead against his and rocked into him. She closed her eyes as she stretched to accommodate him, letting him fill her. She gasped and his hand flew to her face, cradling her cheek.

"Are you okay?"

She threw her head back and laughed. Of course, she was okay. She was better than okay.

She kissed him on the mouth, the salt of their sweat piercing her tongue. He was wide-eyed as he watched her, their bodies rocking together. There were no more words, they let their eyes and their bodies communicate everything.

Griffin's hands traveled her body; cupping her breasts, running his thumb along the contour of her waist, gripping the small of her back. Each small movement sent stars exploding behind her eyes.

She clenched them closed, trying to hold on to the moment, desperate to make it last. She grasped at the last shreds of sanity in a futile attempt to ground herself in the moment, not to let herself be carried away by the pleasure. But she could tell by her own rapid breathing and the way her fingernails pricked his skin that she was close to the edge.

Below her, Griffin tensed, then emitted a long, low groan. He pulled her into him, cocooning her against his body, as they crested on wave after wave of pleasure.

When they'd finally come down, both panting and exhausted, Beth curled against his chest.

She trailed a finger over his skin. "We're definitely doing that again sometime soon."

This time it was his turn to laugh.

CHAPTER NINE

Beth's leg bounced as Griffin drove through downtown Belmont. Her stomach was twisted in a thousand knots. Mabel had howled when they'd left the house. A sound so mournful it had nearly ripped her heart in two.

She glanced at Griffin, who gripped the steering wheel tightly.

"If you don't feel comfortable leaving Mabel, it's really okay. My friends will understand."

She'd been nervous enough to invite him. He already knew Ryan, but meeting the rest of her friends was a big step. Maybe they weren't ready.

He gave her a tight smile. "Mabel will be fine, I promise. She loves Sarah. I think it was just the combination of seeing both of us leave together that set her off. She hates to miss out on anything fun."

A lump lodged in her throat. "Does she normally get upset when you leave?" Beth still couldn't shake the guilt.

He reached for her hand and squeezed it. "It's separation anxiety. It does happen sometimes, but Sarah knows how to handle it."

His jaw worked. "According to the books and the experts, she won't get past it unless I do leave sometimes. Even though it's hard."

Beth nodded. Hard was an understatement. It freaking sucked.

His phone pinged and he motioned to it. "Go ahead and open it. Twenty dollars says Sarah let her do something I'd never allow and she's already forgotten all about us."

She took his phone and swiped to unlock it. Sure enough, there was a photo of Mabel squirting whipped cream from the can directly into her mouth.

She slumped back against the seat. Thank God. The sound of Mabel's cries in her ears would have haunted her all night.

Being a parent was hard. How did he do it?

"So you don't allow her to eat whipped cream straight from the can?"

"Definitely not." He grimaced. "I learned long ago not to pump a child full of sugar at night."

She giggled. Mabel was a firecracker on a normal day. Mabel on sugar had to be terrifying.

She looked up and started when she realized they were at the intersection of Glendale Avenue and Riley Street.

"You should take Talbot instead of Glendale." She tried to keep her tone light and breezy. She hated driving past the storefront for her old business, the stained-glass studio, which had been turned into a chain housewares store.

His brows furrowed, but he kept his eyes on the road. "Okay."

She fidgeted as she waited for him to ask why. She hadn't told him about the bankruptcy yet. The timing had never seemed right.

Luckily, he let her odd request pass. "So tell me about this piñata?" he asked.

She glanced into the backseat, where he'd helped her load the papier-mâché monstrosity. Building it had been harder than she'd expected, but it was her contribution to the surprise party and she'd spent days working on it. Even Ainsley had pitched in.

"When we were eight, Kate had a piñata for her birthday. Some other girl broke it open, I can't remember who, and Kate cried. She was heartbroken. For her next few birthdays her dad bought two piñatas and would save one for us to whack when all the other guests had left. She grinned at the memory. It was so good to have Kate back in Belmont and to see her happy. Finally.

"And you always let her be the one to break it," Griffin said.

"Of course." The whole point of an extra piñata was to let Kate have the satisfaction of smashing it open. Everyone needed a chance to smash something, then binge on candy. It was cathartic for the soul.

He squeezed her hand again. "So why is the piñata a camel or a llama or whatever the heck that is?"

"Alpaca." Designing an alpaca piñata had been a flipping nightmare, but seeing Kate's reaction would be worth it. "She's scared of them."

His eyebrows lifted. "You made her an alpaca because she's scared of them? I never thought I'd say this to you, but you are one sick, twisted individual."

She giggled. "She's scared of them and now she gets to beat the heck out of one with a stick. It seemed fitting to me."

Kate would love it. She knew it.

Griffin grinned at her as he turned into the parking lot at the back of the restaurant. He parked, then they climbed out of the car and circled to the front, where the sign said simply SUSHI.

Griffin held the door open for her. Inside, they climbed a narrow set of stairs to the second floor, where James had said they'd find the private dining room he'd reserved.

Ainsley was already there, flitting around a large circular table and straightening place settings. Griffin let out a low whistle and Beth allowed her gaze to travel around the small room. Silver and white streamers were draped from the ceiling, hundreds of helium balloons crowded the air, and the floor was littered with confetti.

"Do you like it?" Ainsley's face was flushed, but her hair and A-line dress were both unruffled.

"Holy cow!" Beth rushed to her and planted a kiss on her cheek. "I can't believe it! This place looks incredible!"

Of course she'd expected nothing less than perfection from Ainsley.

Ainsley sighed, her shoulders relaxing. "Okay, good. I want Kate to feel special."

Beth gave her another squeeze. "She will."

This was why they loved Ainsley, even when her neurotic

planning threatened to drive them all Fruit Loops. She would do anything for the people close to her.

Ainsley released Beth and held a hand out to Griffin. "You must be Griffin. It's great to meet you. I'm Ainsley."

He shook her hand. "Nice to meet you, too. This is really something."

Ainsley glowed as she surveyed the room.

Ryan's footsteps pounded on the stairs.

"I'm here and the party can begin," he announced loudly.

"Nice to see you, man." Griffin clapped him in a hug.

"Griffin Hall, out in the wilds of Belmont after seven p.m. I never thought I'd see this day." Ryan's blue eyes danced.

Griffin laughed. "The things I do for Beth…"

Her face heated.

"Who knew our Bethie could bring out anybody's wild side?" Ryan scooped her into a hug, sweeping her feet off the ground. "How's it going, Short Stuff?"

She wriggled free. "Can we go one night without the short jokes?"

Ryan's brow furrowed. "Then what would we talk about?"

Ainsley stepped in between them. "Beth, did you remember the piñata? Please tell me you didn't forget the piñata."

Her voice rose in pitch.

Beth took her hand and squeezed it in an attempt to soothe her. "I remembered the piñata. It's in the car."

Ainsley wouldn't be able to relax until she saw the pleasure and surprise on Kate's face.

"I'll get it right now." Griffin jangled the keys in his hand as he took the stairs two at a time.

Ryan swept Ainsley into a hug, squeezing her tightly. "You did a great job. This will blow Kate away."

He lowered his head closer to hers and whispered something in her ear. Something Beth couldn't hear.

Her eyes narrowed and she took a step closer. What had he said?

"Don't mess up my hair." Ainsley's voice was muffled against his chest.

He laughed. "I would never dream of it. Now where's the booze? I think we need to get a few drinks in you. Force you to relax."

"I am relaxed." She stepped away from him and caught Beth's eye, then flushed red. Abruptly, she turned and grabbed another handful of confetti.

Weird.

What was up with them?

Griffin returned with the piñata, a mass of beige tissue paper.

Ryan's eyes widened. "What the hell is that?"

Ainsley planted a hand on her hip. "It's an alpaca."

At this, he burst into booming laughter. "You guys are evil. You know that?"

Ainsley shrugged. "It was Beth's idea."

"Oh yeah?" His glance shifted to her. "Bethie, I never knew you had it in you."

Before she could retort, the piercing wail of an alarm emanated from Ainsley's phone.

"Kate's coming!" She punched a button, ending the noise, then smoothed her dress.

Ryan kept his hands clapped over his ears. "Are you trying to make us all deaf?"

Beth couldn't help it. She smirked. That was more like it. Normally, the two of them had a gift for pushing each other's buttons.

Ainsley grabbed her by the arm and tugged. "We all need to get into position. Immediately."

* * *

Griffin sat quietly at the table, between Beth and James, soaking it all in.

"They always talk over each other like this. You have to jump in there if you want to be heard." James leaned toward him and kept his voice low.

He chuckled. "I have a four-year-old daughter, so I know how that can be."

Still, he couldn't help but stare. They were all so easy with one another, so comfortable. The realization was liking ripping off a Band-Aid, only to find a cut not fully healed. He hadn't had a group of friends like that in…years. Since before Mabel was born, probably. And until this very second, he hadn't realized how lonely that could be.

He swallowed hard, banishing the thought. He was here now. With Beth.

"So you own Little Ray?" Kate asked.

There was a lull in conversation as everyone turned their attention toward him. Under the table Beth's hand rested on his leg.

The test had begun. For Beth, her friends were like family. Their approval was vital.

"Little Ray of Sunshine, yeah. I opened it six months ago, almost exactly."

Ainsley slapped a hand down on the table. "Wait, you named your coffee shop after Beth?"

"That's exactly what I said!" Kate burst out.

He turned to look at Beth, who was blushing. A slow smile overtook him. "You know, I'd never thought of that, but you are a little ray of sunshine."

She scrunched her nose, pretending to be annoyed by the "little" part.

He turned his attention back to Kate, whose eyes were glued to him. The intensity of her stare nearly made him shiver.

Instead, he summoned his widest smile. "Technically, it's named for my daughter, but I think she might be persuaded to share the title with Beth."

Mabel loved Beth, but he was still determined to keep her unaware of their relationship for the time being. Tonight, for example, he'd told her they were going to a party with Ryan.

His skin prickled. He wasn't always the best at protecting Mabel, but that didn't mean he'd stop trying. For now, this was the way things needed to be.

"Beth said you're from Ohio? What made you decide to move to Belmont?" Kate leaned forward, resting her elbows on the table.

His lungs constricted. How had he never worked out a good answer to this question? Every once in a while people asked and yet his strategy had never developed beyond avoidance.

He took a long drink of water and tried to remember exactly what he'd told Beth.

"After Mabel's mom…" Something caught in his throat. "I'd been to Belmont a few times and I always really liked it. It seemed like a good place to settle with a kid, start my own business. I found out about the shop, and he was asking a good price." That was the better answer. He needed to stick with that in the future and scratch the mention of Angela.

He looked down at the table to avoid Beth's gaze. He still hadn't told her about Angela. He couldn't bring himself to do it yet.

"Did you know Bob? The guy who used to own your shop? What was the name of that place? We used to go there in high school…" James looked to Ainsley.

"Big Bob's." Griffin was grateful for the turn the conversation had taken.

"*That* place? You own Big Bob's?" Ainsley's eyes lit in sudden understanding.

He nodded, intrigued by Ainsley's misplaced enthusiasm. The restaurant had been a dump when he'd bought it, but gutting it and redecorating had been the catharsis he needed. Plus, he'd gotten a damn good deal.

Given her golden-blond hair and her perfectly coordinated dress, shoes, and jewelry, he had a hard time picturing Ainsley in that rat trap.

"Ainsley had her first kiss there." James winked in her direction.

Ainsley blushed, her face turning a dark shade of crimson.

Kate dropped her fork to the table. "You're kidding. You guys went to Big Bob's in high school? This is blowing my mind a little bit."

Beth's mouth hung open as she stared at Ainsley.

Ainsley huffed. "Fine. I did have my first kiss there. Thank you for spilling that detail, James. We used to hang out at Bob's a lot. James, why did we hang out there?"

He shrugged. "Close to school. Cheap. Oh yeah, and the guy never carded."

No wonder Bob had found himself suddenly out of business and in a rush to sell. He must have finally been busted.

Ainsley snapped her fingers. "Yes! I remember drinking peach schnapps there."

Ryan pulled a face. "Peach schnapps. Gross. Tell us about this first kiss?"

Ainsley toyed with the straw in her water. "Um…there isn't much to tell."

Ryan's eyes gleamed and he leaned toward her. "Then tell us anyway. Who was the lucky gentleman?"

She wrinkled her nose and plunked her elbows down on the table. "Fine. I was sixteen, okay? Which was a little later than I'd been planning. Everyone else had had their first kiss already, my mom had been all over me about it. This guy, Ricky Cline, and I went out with a group one Friday night. We drank just a little bit and then when the mood was right, I kissed him."

Beth gasped. "Ainsley, you kissed him first? This supports my theory that every woman is a feminist. Deep inside, you're a feminist, too."

Ainsley rolled her eyes. "Hardly. I just wanted to get it over with, so I made the first move."

Beth cupped her hands around her mouth and adopted a stage whisper. "Ainsley, what do you think a feminist is?"

Griffin suppressed the urge to laugh.

Kate spoke, as if reciting from memory. "A feminist is a strong woman who knows what she wants and goes for it."

Beth raised a finger in the air. "Exactly! Which makes you, Ainsley, a feminist!"

Her face glowed in triumph, and Griffin wrapped an arm around the back of her chair. Beth was really, truly one of a kind.

Ainsley shrugged. "I can't say I'm crazy about the label, but I never said I wasn't a strong woman who knows what she wants and goes for it. Speaking of, I want to pee, and I'm going to go for it."

She pushed her chair from the table and walked toward the stairs. When they'd heard her heels clack to the bottom, Kate turned her attention to James.

"So where exactly is Scott?" Her face was lined with concern.

"Scott is Ainsley's boyfriend," Beth whispered to Griffin.

"Hong Kong, I think? He's still working on that merger." James toyed with his chopsticks. "I'm worried. It sounds like he might be transferred there permanently."

Beth groaned. "Ainsley can't go to Hong Kong. She would hate it." Her chin wobbled. "And I would miss her."

Under the table, Griffin reached to squeeze her hand.

James shrugged. "I don't know what's going on. In fact, I don't think he's told Ainsley anything about it, either."

"What an ass," Ryan mumbled, with his mouth full.

Kate toyed with the ring on her finger. "That sucks. Does he have any idea how much pressure her parents are putting on her to get married?"

Griffin's gut twisted. He'd been there, done that: the pressure to get married, the pressure to raise his daughter the "right" way. Whatever that entailed. It was part of the reason he'd bought a busted-up restaurant halfway across the country.

It was so much easier to know the right way to do something when you weren't on the inside, living it firsthand, paralyzed by the fear of making a mistake.

James's jaw worked. "Honestly, I don't know, and she made me swear I wouldn't confront him about it. This is one of those times when I'd love to ask him, but I promised her. Meanwhile, her little sister got engaged the other week and for a moment I thought Ainsley was going to go all *Orange Is the New Black* and shank someone."

Kate slapped his arm. "Don't joke about that! Ainsley wouldn't shank anyone."

James smirked. "I meant with a shiv made from a lipstick tube of course."

Kate frowned at him and he leaned to kiss her on the temple. "I'm just kidding. I know you're worried, but Ainsley is stronger than people give her credit for. Marriage is awesome, but it isn't an easy decision, and she'll figure it out. We just need to trust her to make the right decision, and if she gets hurt, we'll be here to support her."

A tender expression crossed James's face as he looked at Kate and laced his hand with hers.

Ainsley's heels clicked against the stairs.

Ryan quickly changed the subject. "You find a new room-mate yet, Beth?"

Next to him, she squirmed in her seat. "Not yet. Sarah wants me to meet her cousin."

Griffin's spine stiffened. He knew Sarah meant well, but he also knew this was a bad idea. Sometimes when you cared about someone you gave them chances they didn't deserve. Chances to hurt you or someone you loved. Look at him. He'd tried to keep Angela in Mabel's life and all it had gotten him was a big, fat custody battle with her parents.

"But?" Kate's eyes searched Beth's.

He kept his mouth clamped firmly shut. If he had to, he'd tell Beth about Angela and everything she'd put them through before she got locked up. But this wasn't the right time.

"She's a convicted felon," Beth said softly.

Kate's eyebrows rose. "Oh, honey. You can't find anyone else?"

Beth gave a helpless shrug. "I haven't looked. Sarah just said she needed help."

Ainsley slid back into her seat. "What did I miss? What are we talking about?"

"Beth is going to move a convicted felon into Kate's old room." Ryan's eyes stayed fixed on Beth, as if he were watching a riveting action scene on TV.

Griffin placed his hand on top of Beth's and squeezed. She leaned into him slightly, her shoulder a soft pressure against his.

James cleared his throat loudly. "So, Beth, Kate tells me you've got a new garden going?"

Next to him, Beth's face lit up. "Yes! And my kale already sprouted, so I hope you're all looking forward to some creative muffins."

Ryan made a face. "Kale muffins. Count me out. I'd rather eat my own vomit."

Ainsley pushed her chair back from the table. "Well, I hate to end that charming dinner conversation, but I'd say it's time for the piñata, don't you think?"

"Piñata?" Kate met Beth's gaze and grinned. "I love piñatas."

"It wouldn't be your birthday without one," Beth replied.

The others stood and followed Ainsley to the other side of the room.

Griffin looped an arm around Beth's shoulders, as if he could physically protect her from her own doubts and worries. "Don't worry about it tonight. You'll figure it out," he said.

He knew, in his gut, that it was true. Beth might be naive and optimistic and hopeful and idealistic, but she was a good judge of character.

From across the room, Kate shrieked, "An alpaca? Thanks a lot, guys, now I'm going to have nightmares!"

Beth's face broke into a smile. "An alpaca bit her in the ass when we were on a field trip to a farm in high school."

He chuckled. No wonder she was scared of the animal.

"And now she'll get her revenge." Beth jumped from the table and he admired her perky butt as she walked away.

She'd make the right decision. And he'd help her, if she needed help.

CHAPTER TEN

Beth stretched in her bed and reached for the ringing cell phone on her nightstand.

"Hello?"

"Hey." It was Griffin's deep voice. Her heart thumped in her chest.

"I hate to ask you this, but Heidi just called in sick. She was scheduled for a double shift, so I have to go in and work today."

"That sucks." He needed to hire more staff, but it was his business and she was determined to stay out of it. *Been there, done that, have the bankruptcy judgment to prove it.*

"Is there any way you're free to watch Mabel? That's a long time for her to hang out at the store and she's been asking when you could babysit again."

She bolted out of bed, with the cell phone still pressed to her ear. Her palms began to sweat. He wanted her to watch his daughter? For an entire day? He was trusting her with his daughter?

"I'd pay you. In real money, of course. I know it's a lot to ask."

Her lungs squeezed tight. *As a babysitter, not a girlfriend.* That line between the two was proving to be a hell of a lot trickier than she'd thought it would be.

"You know I can't take your money."

"Beth." His voice was flat.

"Griffin. This isn't negotiable. I'm not taking your money."

She bit her lip. Did that make it too real? Was it too much like she was trying to be some kind of parental figure?

Her spine prickled. Babysitting she could handle. After all, she'd been babysitting for years and everyone's kids had survived. But pseudo-parenting? Nope. That was a huge responsibility.

He sighed. "Fine. We'll do some kind of exchange then. Services for services."

A flame ignited low in her belly.

He doesn't mean those kinds of services! Again, the line was blurring. She didn't know how much longer they could keep dancing around this issue, but she wasn't in a hurry to face it head-on.

She padded into the bathroom and turned the shower on full blast. "I'm supposed to meet up with Ainsley and Kate today. I'm altering a dress for Ainsley. Is it okay if they stop by your place?"

"Of course. Mabel would love that."

She reached a hand in to test the temperature of the water.

"Okay. I should be there in thirty minutes then."

There was a long pause. "Thank you. I know this isn't a small favor and I really appreciate your help."

Her heart pitched. She got the feeling that he didn't have a lot of support in Belmont. And she sensed he wasn't used to asking for favors. "I'm happy to spend time with Mabel. Really."

It was just babysitting, she told herself. She could totally babysit.

* * *

A few hours later, Beth sat on the sofa thumbing through a book of short stories when there was a rap on the door.

She jumped to her feet. Mabel would nap for only another fifteen minutes or so. She had to fit Ainsley's dress before Mabel woke up.

Beth jerked open the door, hugged Kate and Ainsley, and ushered them into the hall. "Come on in. There's a bathroom down here, so Ainsley can try on her dress and we can get it pinned. Once Mabel wakes up there will be paint and crayons and sticky fingerprints everywhere."

Straight pins and four-year-olds didn't strike her as a good combination. And when it came to Griffin's daughter, she had to be especially careful not to accidentally maim her.

Kate raised an eyebrow. "So, babysitting? For the boyfriend?"

"Yup, babysitting." She ducked her head, avoiding Kate's gaze.

It was too complicated to get into now and knowing Kate, she was geared up for some best-friend psychoanalysis.

Ainsley glanced back and forth between them. "Oh. Are we going to talk about this now? Should I get the popcorn?"

Beth nudged her in the direction of the bathroom. "Nope. We're not talking about this now. Mabel will be awake soon and trust me, you don't want her to touch that dress."

Ainsley scurried into the bathroom.

"Thanks for doing this on such short notice. It's really important that the dress be perfect. My mom was wearing it when my dad proposed to her," she called through the door.

Beth's heart rate sped. Was Ainsley expecting the dress to work its magic again?

She caught Kate's eye and stepped into the kitchen, pulling Kate behind her.

"Is Scott going to propose?" she whispered.

Kate shrugged. "I have no idea. He planned this fancy dinner for her next Friday, so I think she's expecting it."

A sick feeling came over her. Did Ainsley really want to marry him? Was she actually going to move to Hong Kong?

The bathroom door clicked open and a few seconds later Ainsley stepped into the kitchen, red satin swirling around her legs.

Beth gasped. "Wow." She'd always loved vintage clothes, but Ainsley's dress was particularly stunning.

Kate's eyes went wide. "You look gorgeous."

Ainsley gave a faint smile. "Thanks. It's special to my family. My mom wore it the night my dad proposed and my sister wore it to her anniversary dinner the week before her fiancé proposed."

A small jolt of fear traveled down Beth's spine. She closed her eyes and forced herself to take a deep breath. She altered clothes for people all the time. This wasn't any different, even if the dress held some kind of proposal-inducing magic.

She grabbed her measuring tape and pincushion, then backed up a few feet to survey her friend. "What were you thinking in terms of alterations?"

The fit was already close to perfect.

Ainsley pointed at her chest with one French-manicured fingernail. "If you could lower the neckline here, narrow the bands around the upper arms here, and maybe tuck the waist in half an inch."

Suddenly her face paled. "It's our anniversary and he's flying back and taking me to dinner at Jean Luc's. That's a sign, right?"

Beth dropped her gaze to the pincushion. What if Scott didn't ask Ainsley to marry him? She'd be heartbroken.

Kate wrapped an arm around Ainsley's shoulder. "No matter what, you'll look gorgeous."

Beth gritted her teeth. No good would come out of saying this out loud, she reminded herself. But the words came bursting out anyway. "Do you *want* to marry him?"

Ainsley tensed. "Of course! I always pictured myself getting married before thirty, first kid at thirty. I've been looking at houses in the Point. For when we move back."

"But do you want to marry Scott? Do you want to move to Hong Kong with him?" Her voice was stronger this time.

Ainsley fidgeted, and Beth almost regretted her words. Almost. Once Ainsley married Scott and moved halfway across the globe it would be too late.

Kate took Ainsley's hand and squeezed it. "I would really miss you if you moved to Hong Kong."

Ainsley's eyes filled. "I don't want to move, but I also don't see a way around it. I'm sure Scott's going to take the job, and if he proposes to me, why would I say no?"

Beth gripped the cushion too hard and pricked the pad of her thumb.

She reached for Ainsley's other hand. "No matter what you decide, we'll support you. We just want you to be happy."

Her throat tightened. *I just don't want you to think you have to get married to be happy.* It took all her strength to swallow the words. Ainsley already knew that. She didn't have to say it aloud.

Ainsley dabbed under her eyes, careful to preserve her flawless makeup. "Since we're having heart-to-hearts, are we going to talk about you and Griffin? The fact that you're at his house watching his kid while he works?"

Beth nearly choked. Described like that, she sounded like some kind of fifties housewife.

"They're short-staffed at Little Ray. There was an emergency and he needed a babysitter. And I am a kick-ass babysitter."

Kate raised an eyebrow. "Oh, I know you're great with kids, but what does it mean?"

She flinched. It wasn't like she hadn't thought through all the possible repercussions and hidden meanings. She'd just decided to ignore them. For now.

"I admit, things between us are intense. Like really, crazy chemistry. But he has a daughter and he lost his wife. I don't think either of us is ready for things to become serious fast. And Mabel doesn't know anything about it, so keep your lips zipped."

Kate made a zipping motion over her mouth.

Ainsley, on the other hand, opened hers. "Well, I saw the way he looked at you at Kate's party, and I'm pretty sure he's halfway in love with you already."

Beth's face heated.

Kate burst into laughter. "Ainsley said it, I didn't."

They were kidding, right? There was no way he could be in love with her already. Besides, they didn't know Griffin the way she did. He wasn't one to put his emotions on display.

Upstairs, a door slammed shut, then footsteps pounded on the stairs.

"Shit. Mabel's awake, and I didn't finish your dress yet." She glanced at the pincushion in her hand.

The footsteps stopped right behind her.

"Wow."

She spun to see Mabel, staring openmouthed.

"Mabel, these are my friends, Kate and Ainsley."

Mabel nodded solemnly. "They're your best friends."

She grinned. "You're right. They are my best friends."

Mabel pointed a finger at Ainsley. "Are you a princess?" Her voice was hushed.

"I wish I was, honey." Ainsley's expression lightened.

Mabel frowned. "Well you look like a princess to me."

Ainsley broke into a smile. "Thanks, kid. I needed that."

Beth gripped Mabel's shoulders and carefully steered her around Ainsley and to her seat at the kitchen table. "I need to finish working on Ainsley's dress, but why don't you sit here with Kate and draw some more pictures." They'd started their own children's book that morning. Beth was in charge of the writing, and Mabel was the illustrator.

"Okay." Mabel climbed into the chair, her eyes still glued to Ainsley.

Beth turned back to Ainsley and worked quickly, folding fabric and slipping pins into position. Even if the dress wasn't good luck, Ainsley deserved to look and feel perfect.

When Beth was finished, she stood and stretched her arms over her head. "All right. You're good. Just zip it back into the bag and hang it in the back of Martha. I should be able to finish it in a few days."

Ainsley beamed at her, then grabbed her hand and squeezed it. "Thank you. You're the best."

She stepped carefully into the bathroom and closed the door behind her.

When Beth turned back to the kitchen table, Mabel sat in Kate's lap leafing through pages of brightly colored drawings with bold text. She stopped at a piece of paper covered with a round, green pig. "Then the pig was flying up and over the mountain!" she said.

Kate glanced at Beth. "Did you write out this story with her?"

"Yeah." Beth poured a cup of coffee and sat next to them at the table. "It was Mabel's idea though, wasn't it May?"

Mabel flashed her a toothy grin. "I like pigs. They're cute."

Good thing Mabel didn't know where bacon came from. She'd have enough time for existential guilt when she was an adult.

Kate fingered the page. "This is really amazing. You should do something with it."

Beth stirred her coffee. "Like what?"

"Like send it to a publisher. I'm sure James's mom knows someone. She could call in a favor."

Beth wrinkled her nose. That sounded serious. The book was supposed to be for Mabel, just for fun.

"What's a pub licker?" Mabel pressed hard on the marker, scrubbing it across the page.

"A publisher makes stories into books and sells them," Beth explained.

"So then other kids can read it?" Mabel's eyes grew wide. Then again, it couldn't hurt to try.

Ainsley came back into the kitchen, poured herself a cup of coffee and slid into a seat. "So what are we up to?"

"Coloring." Mabel's marker strayed from the page and left a giant red streak on the wooden table.

Ainsley grabbed a tissue and rubbed at it, but Beth waved her off. "It's fine. If you clean it now, she'll do it all over again. It comes off at the end with some Lysol."

Ainsley tilted her head to the side and examined Beth. "Well look at you, Mrs. Doubtfire. When I have kids, I'm going to need you to walk me through this kind of stuff."

Across the table, Kate giggled. "Wasn't Mrs. Doubtfire a man?"

Ainsley rolled her eyes. "You know what I mean."

"I'm pretty sure she also burned her boobs," Beth added.

Ainsley took a long sip of coffee. "That's a problem I can't help you with."

With a grin, Beth shoved her chair back from the table. "I think today calls for some muffins. What kind of muffins should we make, May?"

She might as well get a jump on the next day's orders while Mabel was occupied.

Mabel's attention remained focused on the picture in front of her, a pig dancing with a donkey. "Banana walnut coffee gummy bear jelly bean!"

Kate shuddered and Beth had to swallow a laugh.

"Let's stick with banana walnut for today, kiddo."

Fifties housewife be damned. She had a business to run.

* * *

It took all Griffin's energy to lift one foot and put it in front of the other. Just a few more steps and he would be home.

His body demanded that he fall straight into bed, but his mind was filled with visions of Beth. Her tousled hair, her sculpted butt, and her sparkling eyes.

His blood heated. The thought of her was better than an IV of caffeine. Suddenly his entire body was alive and humming with expectation.

He twisted his key in the lock and pushed the door. The scent of roasted meat hit him square in the face and he nearly started to drool.

He strode through the hall and into the kitchen, where he

found her sitting at the table. "You cooked for me."

She glanced up from the pages spread in front of her and grinned at him. The light in her eyes hit him straight in the gut and sent him reeling. *Holy shit*. He'd spent all day imagining her, but when she looked up at him like that? The reality of her far surpassed his best daydream.

He swallowed hard. He was falling. He'd told himself he'd take things slowly and give them all time to adjust, but the follow-through was proving a hell of a lot harder than he'd expected.

"I made pot roast. And muffins. The ones on the counter are for you, the ones in the boxes are for work. Mabel already ate. Then she fell asleep in a pile of Legos. She passed out right on top of them. Which I don't get, because have you ever stepped on one? It's like a form of torture. I think she has a future in the CIA."

He strode over to her and pulled her into his arms, then kissed her hard on the mouth. She tilted her head back, inviting more, and threaded her hands through his hair.

He had to force himself to end the kiss, to step back. "Thank you. For making me dinner. It's exactly what I needed tonight."

She rubbed her palm over his upper arm. "Of course. I couldn't let you and Mabel starve, could I?"

His chest tightened. Here he was, after a long day at work, arriving home to a home-cooked meal and a sleeping daughter. And it felt right.

He scrubbed a hand across his face. He was fighting a losing battle. No matter how many times he told himself to move slowly and be cautious for Mabel's sake, he couldn't resist

Beth's sweetness. He sighed. What did that say about him as a father?

"You seem tired. Long day?" She turned to grab a plate from the counter and filled it with food from the stove.

He slumped into a seat at the table. "Tired doesn't even describe it. I feel like I've been beaten into submission. Even coffee can't fix me now."

Beth put the plate in front of him and sat in the wooden chair opposite. "Do you want me to tuck you into bed? Mabel and I wrote a story together. I could read it to you before you go to sleep."

Mabel and I wrote a story together. An ache filled his chest and he dropped his gaze to the food.

"Griffin?" Her voice was soft, tentative.

What is going on with me? He was tired, just tired. And grateful.

But the pot roast reminded him of home, when he'd been a kid. And it broke open something inside of him. "You know, when I was younger, I had this idea that I was going to be someone important or do something important."

Beth nodded, her attention fixed on him.

"I was going to be a famous rock star. Music was the one thing I was really good at. I've always loved it." He didn't know why he was telling her this, but now that he'd started he couldn't stop.

"Shepherdsville is a really small town. Most people own farms that get passed down through generations. When they found oil a lot of people sold their farms, but still everyone moves back home and works in Shepherdsville after college."

Her brown eyes were warm, filled with understanding.

"I hated that. I didn't want to be boring like them, like my parents and their friends and everyone else I knew. I wanted to be interesting and to have adventures."

Her lips curved upward. "I don't think anyone would call you boring."

He shoveled a bite into his mouth and chewed, buying himself a moment to think. He didn't quite know how he'd wound up walking down memory lane.

He grinned back at her. "I could say the same to you."

There was a long silence.

"Also, this is amazing. I can't believe you made it."

She smiled and watched as he inhaled the food on his plate. When he'd finished he pushed his chair back from the table and stood.

An idea sent his blood thrumming through his veins. "Would you like to see my music room?"

He kept his instruments in his office upstairs, locked in a closet where Mabel couldn't get to them unsupervised. Someday he'd teach her to play them all, if she wanted.

Beth practically leaped from her chair. "Yes. I'd love that."

He grinned. He'd been considering the invitation all week, waiting for the right time. The room represented his core, the essence underlying everything he was.

And he was going to show it to her. His heart pounded.

"Come on." He grabbed her hand and led her up the stairs. When they reached his office, he let her in and closed the door behind them.

He unlocked the closet and pulled the guitar case out, leaving the closet door open. Then he sat on the leather love seat and began to play. He sang a few lines about a beautiful woman, making them up as he went along.

Her laughter tickled the air, sending ripples of satisfaction washing over him. This was perfect. Even better than he'd hoped.

"Amazing! And very different from anything I heard you play with Thorny Lemon. What other instruments do you have? What's that one there?" She pointed to the ukulele.

His breathing accelerated. She was genuinely interested. Not because he was a rock star, but because she wanted to experience his love of music.

He caught himself staring at her and shifted his attention to the ukulele. "Excellent choice. Let me show you." He pulled it from its case, strummed a few chords and sang a few more lines about a beautiful woman.

Her face glowed, her expression rapt as she watched him. Happiness filled him until he thought he might burst. Why had he waited so long to share this with her?

"Here. Why don't you try." He lifted the strap and placed it over her head.

God she looked incredible. How had he never imagined how perfect she'd look with an instrument in her hands? It was like his own personal fantasy come to life—if she'd been wearing clothes in his fantasy. But for now, this would do.

He took a deep steadying breath. Her fingers were small and delicate in his grasp as he positioned them on the neck of the instrument. He reached around her with his right arm, cocooning her against his chest while he showed her how to strum with the pick. Her closeness sent a shiver down his spine and it took all his willpower to focus, but thirty minutes later she'd mastered a simple song.

He reluctantly unwrapped his arms from around her to clap. "I'm impressed. Seriously."

She twisted to look at him over her shoulder.

"Can we play a duet?" Her eyes danced with excitement.

The words sent his nerve endings buzzing. *A duet.* It might be the sexiest thing a woman had ever said to him. He grinned at her and whipped out his mandolin.

He counted her into the song and watched her as she played, her dark curls spilling over her face as she focused on the placement of her fingers.

When the song was finished, he set down the mandolin, pulled her onto his lap and buried his head in her neck, tasting the sweetness of her skin. She let out a squeal and squirmed for a second, before she pressed her lips to his and pressed her tongue into his mouth. Adrenaline pumped through his body.

With one hand, he carefully lifted the ukulele over her head and set it in its case. Then he stood and scooped her off of the sofa and into his arms.

"I think it's time for me to tell you a bedtime story," he said.

She snuggled into his neck. "Is it going to have a happily ever after? Those are the kinds of stories I like."

He chuckled. "Maybe. I tell excellent ghost stories, too."

"No." Her voice was low and steady. "Happy endings only."

His heart rate sped and he lowered his mouth to hers, kissing her slowly.

When they ended the kiss, his breathing was ragged. "You win."

She grinned up at him as he carried her down the hall and laid her onto his bed.

Tonight he was all about the happy ending.

CHAPTER ELEVEN

Beth took another sip of her homemade kombucha before she stood and brushed the dirt off her jeans. Griffin had been called into Little Ray again, so she'd offered to watch Mabel at her house.

Her legs tingled as the feeling returned to her feet, which only exacerbated the fact that she desperately had to pee.

She held her hand out to Mabel, who sat cross-legged in Beth's sandy backyard. "Let's go inside for a second. I need to use the bathroom."

Mabel shook her head. "No, thank you. I'm busy."

Mabel was positioning her dolls in preparation for a tea party.

She glanced at the half-empty bottle of kombucha. They were definitely going to need more tea.

She planted her hands on her hips. "Sorry, miss. I'm not comfortable leaving you out here alone. I'll only be thirty seconds."

She twisted her legs together. Another minute and she'd pee herself.

Mabel didn't look up from the dolls. "No, thank you."

Beth hopped in place. Her eyes darted through the backyard. There was a privacy fence, so no one could see in, but she didn't want to teach Mabel it was okay to pee outside. Plus, she counted herself a member of the toilet paper fan club. Some amenities were really necessities.

"Mabel Hall. You need to come inside right now."

This time Mabel looked at her, but she quickly returned to her toys. "You're a big girl, you can go by yourself."

She nearly laughed, but bit the inside of her cheek to hold it back. She was going to pee herself before she got Mabel inside. *Some adult role model I am.*

"Fine." She scanned the yard again. Her large wooden garden boxes, overflowing with vegetables. A six-foot-tall privacy fence. Latched gates. She'd be in and out of her house in ninety seconds and there wasn't much Mabel could get into in the meantime. "I'll be right back. Do not, under any circumstances, move. Do you hear me? Not even if you see Santa and he promises you a pony. Don't move your butt from this spot."

Mabel ignored her.

She half-ran half-waddled into the house and down the hall to the bathroom. There was a small window around shoulder height, so she could see into the yard. She checked on Mabel, then squatted.

As soon as she was done she popped up and looked out the window.

No Mabel. The dolls were there, under the tree, but no Mabel.

What part of don't move your butt did she not understand?

She sprinted out the back door and glanced around the yard. She'd probably gone to the side, out of eyeshot.

"Mabel?" Her voice carried a note of warning.

She trotted to the side yard. The gate was unlatched and hung halfway open.

Shit. Had it been open before? Or had Mabel opened it? Could she even reach the latch?

Her lungs ached and her heart pounded. She tore through the gate, yelling Mabel's name.

In the front yard, the street was quiet. Half of the houses were unoccupied in the off- season. She twisted her head left, then right, frantically searching for any sign of Mabel.

Her mouth went dry, and a wave of dizziness slammed into her. Oh God. Where could she have gone?

"Mabel!" Her voice was high-pitched and frantic now.

Still no response. She yanked her cell phone out of her back pocket and fumbled with it, her palms sweaty.

She dialed Griffin.

It rang six times, then switched over to voice mail. Her throat constricted, making it hard to suck in a full breath.

"Griffin. I, um." She burst into tears. Her voice was shaky as she tried to choke out the words.

"I can't find Mabel. She was in the yard and I went inside for a minute." Oh God. Why had she gone inside?

"I'm going to call the police right now, but you need to come here as soon as you can. Please. I'm so sorry."

She clenched her eyes closed and took a shuddering breath.

She'd call the police. They'd find Mabel. Belmont wasn't that big after all.

She punched the three buttons. Nine. One. One. The line rang once.

"Nine one one. What's your emergency?"

Her fingers gripped the phone so hard she thought her knuckles might break. "My name is Beth Beverly. I live at one zero eight Willow Drive. My boyfriend's four-year-old daughter was in the backyard and she disappeared. I was only gone for a second."

Tears burned her eyes. How could she have taken her eyes off of Mabel, even for a second?

The dispatcher's tone was calm. "Okay, ma'am. I'm sending a unit right now. Can you tell me what she looks like?"

She recited Mabel's description. Blond hair, brown eyes. Today she'd plaited Mabel's hair in French braids and she was wearing a unicorn T-shirt.

"The officers will want a picture of her when they arrive, so we can put it on the Amber Alert."

Amber Alert? Her heart felt as if it would claw its way out of her body.

"Can you think of anyone who might have taken her?"

"What? No!" Why would anyone take Mabel?

"What's your boyfriend's custody situation? With his daughter's mother?"

She sucked in a breath. "His wife died."

"Any other family? Anywhere she would go?"

She bit her lip. "I don't think so. I'm not sure."

The clack of keyboard keys sounded on the other end.

"Okay, honey. I have a unit that's maybe a block from your house. They should be there in a second. In the meantime, I'll stay on the line with you, okay?"

She started to hyperventilate. Where was Griffin? Where was Mabel? He would never forgive her. Losing someone's child was unforgivable.

Her eyes burned as she tried to stay calm. The officers would have questions. She couldn't lose it. She needed to answer their questions and help find Mabel.

Out of the corner of her eye, she saw blue lights flashing.

Thank God. The police were here. Whatever it took, she would find Mabel.

* * *

Griffin slammed the car into Park and flew from the driver's seat.

He sprinted to an officer who was speaking with a sobbing Beth.

"What happened?" Griffin blurted the words without waiting for anyone to acknowledge him.

The officer turned to address him. "Mr. Hall? I'm Detective Blanton."

He shook the balding man's hand quickly. "Where's Mabel?"

"Ms. Beverly ran inside to use the bathroom. She could see Mabel from the window when she uh…" he hesitated, "sat down. When she stood up a few seconds later, Mabel wasn't within view. She went around to the house and found the gate open."

He clenched his fists. Fuck. This couldn't be happening. He couldn't lose his daughter.

Beth's tear-filled eyes pleaded with him, but he couldn't bring himself to meet her gaze.

His chest heaved as he struggled to catch his breath. Right now he cared about finding Mabel only.

Detective Blanton tapped his pen on his notebook. "Ms. Beverly provided us with a selfie Mabel took today. I've sent that out, along with a description of her. Can you think of anyone who might want to take Mabel?"

His blood ran cold. *Angela.*

"I'd like to speak with you alone." The words were like ashes in his mouth. Next to him, Beth's entire body went stiff.

He clenched his jaw. He didn't have time to explain to her. All that mattered was Mabel.

The detective's eyebrows lifted. "Sure. Ms. Beverly, why don't you go with the officers and search the neighborhood."

She turned to Griffin and her red-rimmed eyes met his. "I'm so sorry."

His gut wrenched. What the hell was he supposed to say to her?

He bowed his head. "I know."

She clasped her hands in front of her and rocked on her feet, as if she wanted to touch him, but couldn't.

The detective motioned to another officer. "Ms. Beverly is going to go with you. I'm going to get some more information from Mr. Hall."

He couldn't look at her as she walked away. Instead, he took a step closer to the detective and lowered his voice.

"Mabel's mother lives in Ohio. Or at least she was living in Ohio. Last time I checked she was incarcerated. Drugs. But she's probably out by now. I won a really nasty custody battle with her parents about a year ago."

The officer scribbled frantically. "I'm going to need names and addresses. We'll send the police department in Ohio to check at their houses."

Nausea rose in his throat. So Angela and her parents would know that Mabel had gone missing. Great. There'd be another custody petition on his doorstep tomorrow.

Something splintered in Griffin's temple. He hunched over with his palms on his knees, willing the pain to pass.

This can't be happening.

Detective Blanton set a rough hand on his shoulder. "If Mabel got out of the yard on her own and is on foot, she can't have gone far. I'll call all of our beach-patrol guys to look for her. They know this area and the boardwalk like the back of their hands. If she's around they'll find her."

He racked his mind desperately. *Mabel.* Where would she have gone? What could she be doing?

"Then I need to look for her, too."

Detective Blanton gave a brisk nod. "Just give me those names and addresses and you're welcome to join the search party."

He rattled off the address for Angela's parents. Wherever she was, they'd probably know.

"So I can go? I can look for Mabel now?" His leg muscles flexed. He was ready to cover some ground.

"Yes. I'll call you on your cell phone if we hear anything. Make sure it's on."

Griffin set off at a jog in the direction of the beach. He had to find Mabel. The alternative was unimaginable.

At the end of the block, he came to a stop, looking in both directions. Which way now? His hands shook. How the hell were they supposed to find her?

He crossed the street at a brisk speed and trotted aimlessly while his heart thudded in his chest.

A flash of white in an alley caught his attention.

"Mabel?" His voice was strained. "Mabel?" He yelled louder this time.

A blond head popped up from behind a trash can. "Hi, Daddy! Look what I got!"

He ran toward her at full speed, adrenaline flooding his body. When he reached her, he swept her into his arms and crushed her to his chest.

A faint *mew* sounded.

What the hell?

Mabel's small hand shoved him back from her. "Careful! You're smushing the kitty!"

He loosened his grip and looked down to see a tiny black ball of fluff in her arms. A filthy, tiny black ball of fluff.

He narrowed his eyes. "Mabel, where did you find the kitty?"

She avoided his gaze. "Well…"

With one finger he tilted her chin so her eyes met his.

"So, I was playing…with Beth…in the yard. And she had to pee, so she went inside and then I heard a *mew* and I saw a kitty. And oh, Daddy, I've always wanted a kitty. Can we keep the kitty?"

His knees gave way and he crumpled to the ground, still cradling Mabel as she clutched the kitten. She'd wandered off for a kitten!

Heaving sobs racked his shoulders as he struggled to catch his breath. She was here. She was safe.

Mabel stared at him, wide-eyed. "Uh-oh."

He chuckled. "Uh-oh is right."

He stood, lifting Mabel and the kitten into his arms. Then he trudged back in the direction of Beth's house. It was time to call off the search team.

CHAPTER TWELVE

Beth's vision blurred as she stumbled down the boardwalk. Where was Mabel? What if she was lost and scared? *Please don't let her be scared. Please let her be safe. Please let her come home.*

The trill of her phone made her jump.

"Hello?"

Griffin was breathless on the other end. "I found her, she's fine. You can come back to the house now."

Her heart soared. *Mabel is found! Mabel is safe!* "Where was she? Are you sure she's okay?"

"She saw a kitten, so she followed it."

She sank to her knees and a sob rose in her throat. Mabel loved animals. Of course she'd made friends with a stray kitten.

"I'll see you in few minutes." His voice was gruff.

Her stomach dropped and her eyes burned. Mabel was safe, but how could he possibly forgive her? She'd lost his daughter, the most important person in his life. She had no right to his trust.

It took all her effort to push herself back to standing. Her feet were leaden as she walked back to the patrol car.

She allowed the uniformed officer to open the rear door, guide her to the seat, and close it behind her.

Her mind was numb as the small businesses and shops scrolled by. Seagulls squalled and dodged low on the board-walk, looking for dropped food.

A kitten.

Tears of relief spilled over, soaking her face. Mabel was fine.

When they pulled up to the house, Griffin stood in the middle of the sidewalk with Mabel clutched to his chest.

As if in slow motion, she cracked the car door open and walked toward him. He turned to watch her, his lips pressed together in a grim smile.

Her throat tightened and she had to work to swallow.

"Beth!" Mabel wriggled until Griffin set her on the ground. She sprinted over and wound her arms around Beth's shins.

"I'm sorry."

Beth crouched in front of her. She drank in May's image, running her hands over her soft hair.

Mabel placed a small hand on Beth's cheek. "I really am sorry, I promise."

She grabbed May and clutched her to her chest. "I'm just glad you're okay."

Mabel grabbed her hand and tugged her in the direction of one of the uniformed officers. Beth could feel Griffin's eyes burning into her, but allowed herself to be led by Mabel.

Her throat tightened. She didn't know if she could bear to hear the things he must want to say to her right now.

The officer held a ball of black fuzz in his cupped hands.

Mabel pointed to it. "I found a baby kitty."

Beth peered into his hands at the mud-streaked kitten. Her heart squeezed. "You did find a kitten."

Griffin joined them, his arms stiff at his sides.

Beth shivered. Was he deliberately trying to avoid touching her?

"Mabel, we should get home." His voice was sharp.

Beth fixed her gaze forward, on the kitten, desperately trying not to look at him. Her heart was shriveling inside her chest. She couldn't face the disappointment she knew she'd find in his expression. She swayed, but managed to stay on her feet.

Mabel's face crumpled. "But I need to take care of the kitty. It's my kitty!"

Griffin's fists clenched. "I know you want a kitty, but I bet this kitty belongs to someone. We need to try to find his home. And you know we don't have time to take care of a kitty."

Mabel's chin wobbled and Beth found herself reaching for the kitten. "I'm going to try to find his family May. And if I can't find them, I'll take care of him for a while, okay?"

Mabel's expression turned solemn as she lifted her eyes to Beth. "His name is Black Kitty."

Beth nodded and gently accepted the kitten from the officer, pressing it against her chest.

Finally, she glanced at Griffin. His expression was stony.

Her throat thickened, making it impossible to force out words. Should she apologize again? Would it even make a difference now?

His eyes flicked to her face and his expression softened slightly. Then he reached for Mabel's hand. "May, say goodbye to Beth, please. And go to the car. I'll be there in a minute."

Mabel gave a dramatic sigh, then lifted a hand and waved. "Bye, Beth! See you later. Thanks for watching my kitty." She eyed the cat longingly.

"Bye, Mabel." Beth couldn't muster more than a whisper.

The moment Mabel was out of hearing range, he turned to her.

Her heart raced as she clutched the kitten in her hands. Maybe he could forgive her.

A sob burst out of her throat. "I'm so sorry. I can't even tell you how sorry I am. I'm so sorry."

He blinked hard, before his eyes clouded. "I know you are. And I'm not mad at you."

"You're not?" Hope filled her, like a balloon.

His mouth twisted. "I'm not mad. I don't know what I am. Scared shitless, I guess." He shoved a hand through his hair. "I really thought I might have lost her and I can't explain to you how fucking awful that felt."

Her breath caught. She'd been panicked and terrified, too, but it wasn't the same. Mabel wasn't her daughter.

He gripped her shoulders. "I can't lose her. I can't."

She nodded, suddenly mute. After everything he'd already lost, it made her physically ill to think of what she'd put him through.

He dropped his head. "We can't do this, Beth. We can't see each other. It's not because of how I feel about you."

All the air left her lungs.

He clenched his eyes shut. "Or I guess it is because of how I feel about you, because I'm too distracted. You are the most distracting person I've ever met, and I'd be lying if I said I didn't like it, but that's not fair to Mabel. She needs to be the focus of my time and attention, and I don't think I can do that and be in a relationship."

Beth began to shiver.

He cupped her cheek. "You're incredible, but I can't date you and run Little Ray properly and be a good dad. Because I can't just be a dad to Mabel, I have to be the best dad."

Her throat burned as tears spilled onto her cheeks. She'd never want him to put her before Mabel, she just wanted to be with him. Was that so much to ask for?

She swallowed a sob. "I'm so sorry. I really am so sorry."

It was the only thing she could think to say. As if understanding the depth of her regret would make him change his mind.

He leaned toward her and brushed his lips across her forehead. "I'm sorry, too, Beth."

Then he turned and walked away.

* * *

Griffin paced the house, his thoughts racing. Mabel was upstairs in his bed watching a movie. He didn't have the strength to entertain her right now.

Instead he stared at the phone in his hand as the gnawing sensation built in his chest.

Don't call her. He collapsed onto the sofa and dropped his head into his hands. His temple pounded.

Obviously he wasn't ready to date. He wasn't capable of being a boyfriend and a good father at the same time. He'd been fooling himself to think otherwise. He'd let his feelings for Beth blur all the lines he'd drawn for himself, but they'd existed to protect May.

His gut twisted.

He'd almost lost her today, in more ways than one. Thank God she hadn't been hit by a car or wandered into someone's pool or made friends with a kidnapper. And thank God he'd found her before the officers in Ohio had made contact with Angela's parents.

He clenched his fists. He had to be a better father to Mabel. Even if it meant letting go of Beth.

The muscles in his neck seized. How was he just supposed to give her up?

A knock at the door yanked him from his thoughts. His heart leaped, and he pushed himself up from the sofa, crossing the room quickly to peer through the peephole.

Ryan. His shoulders slumped. Of course it wasn't her.

He sighed, then unlocked the door and opened it. At least Ryan was a good distraction. He always kept things interesting.

"Hey, man." Ryan held out a six-pack. "Heard you had a shitty day. Thought you might want some company."

Beth must have told him.

"Thanks." He stepped aside to let his friend in.

"So." Ryan flopped onto the sofa and cracked open a beer. "You want to talk about it?"

A bead of sweat trickled down the back of Griffin's neck. The last thing he wanted to do right now was talk about it.

"Nope." He collapsed into the seat next to Ryan, opened a beer for himself, and propped his feet on the coffee table.

Ryan tilted his head back, resting it on the back of the sofa. "Thank God."

They sat in silence, sipping their beer for a few minutes. Griffin normally didn't drink when Mabel was awake but today demanded an exception.

Ryan broke the silence. "What's the dumbest thing you did when you were a kid?"

Griffin frowned as he thought about it. "I guess that depends what you mean by 'dumb.'" His parents had been pretty pissed when he dropped out of college to go on tour with Thorny Lemon. But technically he hadn't been a kid then, and the whole thing had turned out well enough. They also hadn't been too thrilled when he'd arrived home and announced he was having a baby with a groupie, but again, it had worked out, eventually.

He took another swig of beer. "I once ran into my dad's new tractor with the car, when I was twelve and learning to drive on the farm. Oh, and when I was eight I accidentally shot myself in the foot with a BB gun."

The hazards of growing up in the country.

Ryan chortled.

"You?"

Ryan shook his head. "My poor mother. You have to feel bad for her. I was a terrible kid. The worst. She says I must have had a death wish. When I was two I fell off a fifth-story balcony and smashed my head on the concrete. They flew me to the hospital by helicopter and everyone thought I was going to die, but I turned out fine." He knocked on his head to illustrate.

"When I was sixteen I refused to wear a cup when I played baseball. So of course I got hit in the gnads and, well," he gestured with his beer, "you don't want to know the rest of that story."

Griffin coughed in surprise. "Correct. I don't want to know the rest of that story. In fact, I deeply regret knowing what you've already told me."

Ryan grinned. "And you don't even know the half of it."

Then his brows furrowed. "It's hard to be a single parent, huh?"

Griffin's beer went down the wrong pipe and he almost choked. When he'd finally recovered he gave a grim nod. "Definitely not easy." More like lonely and scary and exhausting.

Ryan frowned. "Yeah, well, I turned out fine. And Mabel will, too."

For the briefest second, his heart lifted. She would turn out fine. Because that was his most important job in life, and he couldn't afford to fuck it up. He refused to fuck it up.

Which meant he had to make safer, better decisions in the future. He sighed and took another pull on his beer. He rubbed at his temple.

Sometimes being a responsible adult freaking sucked.

CHAPTER THIRTEEN

Beth stared at the shelter hours, posted in black on their front door, and clutched the kitten tighter in her lap. Her eyes burned, although she didn't know if it was for lack of sleep or from crying all night.

She swallowed the lump in her throat and gritted her teeth. It was 8:55 a.m. The animal shelter would open in five minutes. And then she'd have to get out of the car, walk up to the front desk, and what? Her lip trembled. She couldn't just leave Black Kitty there.

She sighed and leaned her head back against the seat. Classical music played softly through the radio. She'd thought that might help reassure the kitten, who'd spent the entire night curled against her chest.

Her heart clenched. If nobody had reported Black Kitty missing, then she'd just have to learn to take care of a cat. There was no reason they both had to be alone. The least she could do was take care of the kitten, for Mabel.

Her vision blurred as she glanced at her phone again. No new messages.

He isn't going to call.

He'd said she was too distracting. That he needed to focus on being a father.

It wasn't as if she'd thought dating a man with a child would be a piece of cake. In fact, it still scared the shit out of her. But things between them had felt so natural that she'd managed to convince herself it would be okay. She'd fooled herself into thinking they could handle it together.

She swallowed past the lump in her throat. It would be selfish to try to convince him to change his mind. He was Mabel's dad and he knew what was best for her, which meant there was nothing left for Beth to say. His mind was made up.

Her chest grew tight and she had to force herself to focus on her breathing.

It's okay. It will be okay. They'd been dating for only a few weeks. She'd bounce back. Eventually.

An employee stepped up to the shelter door and flipped the sign to OPEN.

Beth looped her purse over her shoulder and opened the car door, cradling the tiny kitten in one hand.

She had to get in there and get this over with. Rip the Band-Aid off. If Black Kitty did have a family, they'd be missing her.

She headed straight to the front desk, where she found a man with a ponytail and a T-shirt that read BELMONT ANIMAL CONTROL.

She squared her shoulders. "I found this kitten." She extended her hands, the kitten curled into a peaceful, snoozing ball.

He glanced up from the stack of papers in front of him and eyed it. "You found it? Where?"

"Well my, uh," she gulped, "my friend's daughter found her by my house on Willow."

Friend. She nearly burst into tears all over again.

He reached to prod the kitten's nose, eyes, and mouth. Then he shook his head. "Poor thing. It's only a couple of weeks old. It shouldn't be out there on its own."

Her throat grew thick. "Do you think someone's looking for it?"

His eyes snapped to hers, an amused smile playing on his lips. "No. It probably belonged to a stray cat and something happened to the mom. It's lucky you all found it."

Her heart swelled. Mabel had saved the kitten. Literally.

"So what do I do with it?"

He sighed and dropped a hand down on the pile of papers. "You can fill out one of these and we can put it into intake. It'll become available for adoption in ten days, but it's awfully small. We'll have to wait awhile to find it a family and they are exposed to a lot of germs here, so I can't make any promises."

Her heart raced and she shook her head frantically. "But what if I can't leave it? What if it, uh, it has a name and I want to keep it? Do I have to fill anything out or pay someone or what?"

His eyes brightened and he smiled at her. "Then you don't have to do anything. We haven't had any reports for missing black kittens and I can more or less promise you it's a stray. Get it to a vet soon, but in the meantime, congratulations. You have a new kitten."

Her hands shook, but she kept Black Kitty close to her as she nodded. "Well, um, okay. Thanks."

It was only once she was back in the car that the doubt hit her. What in the hell was she supposed to do with a kitten? She needed to call Kate.

* * *

He slammed the pitcher on the counter, sending milk sloshing over the sides. Then he banged the palm of his hand into the side of the computer.

"Goddamn piece of shit computer from hell," he muttered. He could feel the blood vessels pounding in his head. He'd woken up in a bad mood, and Mabel's endless rendition of "Uptown Funk" hadn't helped.

"Whoa, whoa!" Sarah stepped between him and the computer, arms wide as if she were breaking up a fight. "Let the computer live."

He scowled at her and breathed heavily. He was in no mood for her jokes.

She stared at him for a second before she grabbed him by the elbow and dragged him to the back. "What is going on with you?"

His spine stiffened. Sooner or later she'd find out. "Beth and I broke up."

"What happened?" She stepped back to examine him.

"It just didn't work out. There's no way it can work."

Her eyes narrowed. "Please tell me you didn't screw things up."

His pulse throbbed. If anything, he had finally set things right.

The back of his neck prickled. Hadn't he?

"Yeah, I thought so. Sit down." She used her foot to pull a metal stool out from the prep counter. He glared, but sat anyway.

"Tell Auntie Sarah what happened so we can fix it and everyone can stop hiding from you." She patted his shoulder.

"From me?"

She nodded. "Yup. You're giving off the same vibe as a nest of angry hornets and we can't afford to have any more staff members quit."

He gritted his teeth. It wasn't his fault he couldn't find good help.

"Come on now. Spill." She nudged him with her shoulder.

He sighed. Fine. The pressure of holding it in was eating a hole in his stomach anyway. Last night he'd had to pretend in front of Mabel that everything was fine, when really he just wanted to write angry music and crank his amp to full volume.

"I can't do it. Between here and being a dad to Mabel, I can't date. I don't have time, I'm too distracted." He scrubbed a hand over his face. "Mabel disappeared yesterday."

She sucked in a breath. "What? How?"

A knot formed in his stomach. "She disappeared while Beth was watching her. Apparently she found a kitten and decided she needed to save it. But she scared the hell out of me." Suddenly it was hard to swallow.

Sarah rested a hand on his knee. "God. Why didn't you tell me?"

His lungs constricted, but he managed to shrug. "I told

Brian to cover me and drove straight there. And then once I'd found her I just didn't want to talk about it."

"So what does that have to do with dating Beth?" Her voice was gentle.

He gripped the edge of the prep table, the metal indenting into his palms. "Everything. I'm not magic, I can't juggle all these different things. Something has to give, and that something can't be Mabel. It can't be this place. Which only leaves me with one option."

"Huh." She made a sound low in her throat.

The silence that followed was deafening.

She tilted her head to the side, watching him. "I find it interesting that you decided to break up with your girlfriend, a person who makes you happy, instead of hiring more staff."

His blood started to boil again. "It's not that simple and you know it."

Hiring more staff would help, but it wouldn't fix the fact that he didn't have enough time for everything. When it came to Beth he couldn't help himself. He acted selfishly. And there was no room to be selfish when you were a parent.

She huffed. "Don't be ridiculous. Hiring employees will help. And quite frankly, I'm pretty sure you need Beth. You are a much happier, calmer person when she's around. She's basically your equivalent of popping a Xanax."

The pounding in his head grew in intensity. "I want to hire more people. I just can't seem to find anyone who's qualified."

She looked at him for a long moment, as if weighing the danger.

"That's why you have me. First you're going to promote me to assistant manager. Then you're going to hire my cousin Mandi. The least you can do is give her a trial period. And then you're going to give me permission to hire any other staff as needed."

Something inside him unraveled. He was too tired to keep doing everything by himself. He stood and shoved the stool back. "Sure. Fine. Hire and train whoever you want."

Her eyebrows raised. "Really?"

"Yup." The business had grown faster than he'd expected. He was fooling himself to think he could continue to handle every aspect alone.

"Wow." She plopped onto the stool. "That was a whole lot easier than I thought it was going to be. I have all these convincing arguments saved up, but now I don't know what to do with them."

He chuckled and leaned against the counter. "By all means. If it's that important to you, go for it."

At that moment, Cora popped her head around the corner. "Um, Griffin? There's a police officer here to see you."

His spine prickled. A police officer? What did a police officer want with him?

He covered the distance to the partition quickly. Another day, another shit storm.

He came to an abrupt halt before he reached the counter.

Detective Blanton. Was he following up on yesterday? Or had something else happened?

The detective smiled and raised a hand in greeting. "Mr. Hall! I didn't know you owned this place."

Some of the tension in his shoulders eased. At least the detective wasn't here about Mabel.

He plastered a smile on his face. "Detective, what can I do for you?"

Detective Blanton slid a picture to him across the counter. "We had an incident down at the beach today. Some of the locals seem to believe the suspect is a regular here, so we were hoping you can identify him."

He glanced down at it. *Thunder.* His heart lodged in his throat. It was a mug shot of Thunder.

What the hell had he done? Thunder was raggedy, but seemed harmless enough.

Sarah stepped beside him and peered at the photo. "Thunder! What did he do?"

Detective Blanton whipped out his notebook and flipped through a few pages. "According to eyewitnesses he was at the beach this morning, naked as the day he was born, running around with two fists full of tacos."

Griffin's jaw dropped open. This was a joke, right? He had to be kidding.

Beside him Sarah burst into laughter.

The detective raised his eyes to Griffin's. "So you know him?"

His throat grew dry. "Yeah. He comes by around three every afternoon."

He'd already been by today, before the babysitter picked Mabel up and took her home for dinner. His stomach dropped.

Shit. He clenched his fists. "I let that guy around my daughter." His voice came out as a growl.

He was definitely not about to win any father-of-the-year awards. Hell, he'd be lucky if Detective Blanton didn't call Child Protective Services.

Detective Blanton scribbled something in the notebook. "Is it okay with you if I come in around three o'clock tomorrow and see if I can make contact with him?"

"Sure, yeah, whatever you need to do," he muttered. As if the police needed his permission.

The detective flipped the notebook shut. "Good. In the meantime, you and I should have a talk."

His heart tripped, and he anxiously glanced around the dining room. It was 7:00 p.m. on a Wednesday, so at least business was slow. He didn't need his customers to overhear the parenting lecture he was about to receive.

Still, his palms began to sweat when the detective leaned onto the counter and lowered his voice. "I'm a single father, too. My ex and I got divorced three years ago. My son is twelve, and I see him every other weekend. Believe me when I tell you that it doesn't get easier. I don't care how often you get custody of your kid or how much you love her, at least once a day, you'll be convinced you're screwing her up. But you know what? We all feel that way, and most of us are doing a decent enough job."

A lump formed in Griffin's throat, and all he could do was nod.

The detective straightened. "What happened yesterday wasn't your fault. You have to learn to forgive yourself. And forgive the woman, your girlfriend. We all make mistakes. You're a good dad. I can tell." He winked, hitched up his belt, and ambled toward the door.

Griffin cleared his throat. Gratitude washed over him. How could he ever thank the detective for such kind words?

"Detective Blanton, do you want a coffee? For the road?" It was the least he could do.

The detective grinned at him over his shoulder. "Maybe tomorrow."

Next to him, Sarah leaned back against the counter and crossed her arms over her chest. She smirked. "Forgive the woman, huh?"

He stared at her, his mind whirring. As the pieces clicked into place, the tension in his chest eased. The detective was right. He was a good father. He was trying his hardest and even though his hardest would never feel good enough, Mabel was a great kid. So far, she was turning out just fine.

His heart lurched. What the hell had he been thinking, breaking up with Beth? She was the best thing that had happened to him in a long time. Him and Mabel.

He blinked a few times as his thoughts crystallized. He knew what he had to do.

He turned to Sarah. "Can you handle the store for a while?"

She nodded. "Of course. I am the assistant manager, after all."

He rounded the counter and headed for the door as he dug his car keys from his pocket. "Thanks. I really appreciate it."

His pulse raced. He didn't have much time to draft one hell of an apology.

CHAPTER FOURTEEN

Beth stood in the middle of her kitchen, surrounded by dirty bowls and pans. She squared her shoulders and proudly surveyed the chaos. Two hundred and forty muffins baked. When Sunnyside Organic Grocery had called to place a last-minute order, she'd enthusiastically agreed. This wasn't the time for self-pity. She had a business to run.

The doorbell chimed, interrupting her thoughts. It had to be Kate and Ainsley.

"Come in!" she called.

Perfect timing. Now she could procrastinate on washing the dishes, which was the very worst part of baking.

She wiped her hands on a towel and stepped into the hallway to greet them.

Kate, clad in a pencil skirt and silk shirt, immediately pulled her into a hug. "How are you doing?"

Ainsley was holding a vase of tulips and a bottle of tequila.

She set them on the counter, then joined the hug, sandwiching Beth in the middle.

Beth's chest ached and her throat burned. Before she knew it, her breathing was ragged and her cheeks moist.

Kate smoothed a hand over her hair. "I know."

Ainsley tightened her grip around them both, as if she could squeeze the pain away.

When they finally released Beth, she sniffled and wiped her face. "So are we doing shots or what?"

Ainsley watched her with a solemn expression. "We can do whatever you want to do, whatever will make you feel better. But we did bring tequila. You know. Just in case."

Beth squeezed her hand. "Thank you guys for coming by. I really didn't want to be alone tonight."

Kate threw an arm around her shoulders. "You have us. You're never alone."

Her heart squeezed. Of course she had them. But that didn't mean she wasn't alone.

"God, these shoes are killing me." Kate bent to adjust the strap for her heel, lifting one foot into the air and holding on to Beth for balance.

She teetered for a second before she toppled over, knocking Beth onto the floor with her. Good old clumsy Kate.

Beth giggled as she tried to right herself. Confined by her narrow skirt, Kate flopped about on the floor like a fish out of water.

Ainsley laughed as she extended a hand to each of them. Kate grasped the left, Beth grasped the right and Ainsley helped pull them both back to their feet.

"Oh my gosh." Kate heaved, strands of dark-brown hair falling across her face. "I'm sorry. I didn't mean to, um…assault you." She giggled and clapped a hand over her mouth.

This sent Beth into a fresh fit of laughter. Kate always knew how to cheer her up, even when she wasn't trying. Ainsley shook her head at them, grabbed the bottle of tequila and went to the kitchen. When she returned she had three glass tumblers balanced in the palm of her other hand.

"I think we should all toast to Kate and her flawless comedic timing. Even if it is unintentional."

"Anything to cheer up a friend," Kate said.

Beth sighed and slumped against her, letting Kate wrap her in another hug.

They were silent for a long moment.

"He still hasn't called." Beth's voice was soft.

"Then he's an idiot," Ainsley muttered.

Beth's heart twisted. He wasn't an idiot. He was just trying to make the best decision for his daughter.

"I don't know. Maybe he's right. I'm not ready to be responsible for a kid. I mean, God, I lost her yesterday, and I was being careful. I can't guarantee him something like that wouldn't happen again. Maybe it's better that we end it now, before things get too complicated."

Her stomach wrenched. If this was the right thing, then why did she feel so awful?

Kate held her gaze. "Being in a relationship with someone is always complicated and you will always have to make compromises. You have to decide if Griffin altogether, the whole package, is worth it. Will he make you so happy that the compromises and complications don't matter?"

Beth's eyes stung. She'd thought so. But apparently he didn't feel the same way.

"Wow." Ainsley slumped into a chair. "I'm nowhere near as wise as Kate, so...tequila?" She raised the bottle in the air.

There was a loud knock on the door.

Kate raised her eyebrows. "Are you expecting someone?"

Beth's pulse sped. Expecting? No. Not exactly. But there'd been that one shred of hope that had nagged her all day.

"Beth?" Griffin's deep voice carried through the wooden door and into the living room. Her heart leaped. Blood pounded in her ears as anticipation and trepidation washed over her. Finally. He'd come.

She squeezed her eyes shut and sucked in a deep breath, willing her heart rate to slow. Instead, the fluttering grew in intensity.

Something jabbed her in the side and her eyes flew open.

Ainsley stood next to her. "Are you going to let him in? Or should we just leave him out there and let him think about what he did?"

Beth exhaled a sharp bark of laughter. Of course she was going to let him in.

Kate stood and grabbed her purse. "Then that's our cue to get the hell out of here. Even though I haven't gotten to meet the kitten yet."

She raised her voice. "Bye, kitten, wherever you are. For the record, I am your aunt, and I'll be back with treats!"

Ainsley grabbed the bottle of tequila and followed Kate to the door. "I have a feeling I now need this more than you do."

She flashed Beth a weak smile. Scott had pushed his flight and dinner at Jean Luc's back another week and Beth could see the anxiety on Ainsley's face.

Beth's body hummed with nervous energy as Kate yanked the door open. On the other side was a pair of large hands wrapped around a pot, which held a tree. The flowery branches blocked the rest of Griffin from view.

"What the hell?" Kate stumbled, then shot Beth a look over her shoulder. "Um, I think he brought you a tree. That's weird. Oh, I love you, bye!"

Ainsley stopped to stare and shook her head. "I love you, too. Call me if you need tequila!"

They slipped past the tree and were gone.

Griffin set the pot on the porch and hesitated in the doorway. He shifted on his feet, but his eyes were glued to her. "Can I come in?"

She took a few tentative steps toward him, her feet heavy. "Yeah. Of course."

Her tongue was thick in her mouth. All day she'd hoped he would come and now that he was here, she was almost afraid to look at him.

Griffin lifted the pot and heaved it through the door, then set it to one side of the sofa. The fragrant perfume of the blossoms tickled her nose. The branches shot in every direction, taking up a good section of her cramped living room.

She raised her eyes. The image of him, live and in person, with his shaggy, blond hair and his strong shoulders hit her full force. Her breath caught in her throat.

He wrung his hands, his gaze fixed on the tree. "I wanted to get you flowers, but all the cut flowers were dead and I didn't want to get you a dead present, but the florist said there aren't many live flowers this time of year and before I knew it I'd wound up with this."

A lock of hair fell over his face and she was overcome with the urge to brush it away and run her fingers along his jaw. Instead she laced her hands together behind her back.

"I like it."

He let out a harsh breath. "I didn't want to come empty-handed and then I couldn't decide—nothing seemed good enough—and, well…" He gestured to the plant. "I got you a tree."

She giggled at the sheepish look on his face. He had, in fact, bought her a tree.

The lines on Griffin's face relaxed slightly, and he strode toward her and grabbed her hands in his. His thumbs traced over her knuckles, sending a shiver down her spine.

He cleared his throat loudly. "I made a huge mistake. I panicked on every level, and I bailed on you. You deserve better than that, and I'm sorry."

She slumped into him, relief washing over her.

His arms tightened around her as he drew in a ragged breath.

"I'm so sorry, Beth."

She snuggled deeper into his chest. "I'm sorry."

The knot in her stomach released and a wave of tears crashed over her.

He pulled back and looked her in the eye. "There's something I should have told you sooner."

He paused, his throat working.

Her heart sped. This was it. He was going to tell her about Mabel's mom.

"Angela's parents fought me for custody of Mabel. They used my past, the reputation I'd created for Thorny Lemon and they tried to convince a judge that I was unfit as a parent."

His Adam's apple bobbed as he swallowed. "I freaked out yesterday. I thought I'd lose Mabel and I'd prove them all right."

Her body went cold and she clenched his upper arms. "But you didn't lose her, I did!"

Tears poured down her cheeks.

He cradled her face in his hands. "It was an accident. You're incredible with her, and she adores you."

His eyes darkened. "I realized today that I've been trying so hard to live up to everyone's idea of what I should be as a dad, how I should take care of Mabel, that I've forgotten to trust my own instincts. In my head I know that people would tell me to take things slowly and to introduce you to Mabel gradually. But in reality when I'm around you and I see her around you, my gut tells me that's right. Trying to keep the two of you in separate parts of my life feels wrong. I don't think that's the way things are supposed to happen for the three of us."

Relief crashed over her and she buried her face in his chest. He was right. Mabel was an intrinsic part of who he was. She wanted Griffin the whole package, and he wasn't whole without Mabel.

A pang of anxiety shot through her. If they were really going to move forward, if they were going to make this work, there was one more thing she needed to tell him.

"I want you to know that I would never try to replace her mom. I can't imagine what it was like for you and Mabel when she died, but I know I can't replace her, and I don't want you to feel like I'm trying to take her role."

He stiffened and his breathing grew shallow. Her lungs constricted. *Please let him understand*. She didn't need him to pretend Angela had never existed.

The painful silence stretched.

"I can't talk about her." His voice was strained.

Her heart lodged in her throat. "I don't need you to talk about her. I just needed to tell you that. Out loud. So we can move forward together without any misunderstandings."

Whatever he felt, she didn't want him to think he needed to protect her. When he was ready to talk about Angela, she was ready to listen.

He pressed his forehead to hers, although his chest muscles were still tense beneath her palms.

"You are the most incredible woman I think I've ever met." His lips found her, pressing softly and then more urgently. "I hope you know I meant what I said. From now on I want to be able to share you with Mabel, and I want to be able to share Mabel with you."

A wave of emotion crashed over her and tears pricked the corners of her eyes. *Will he make you so happy the compromises and complications don't matter?*

Yes. Griffin Hall was worth it. Whatever "it" was.

CHAPTER FIFTEEN

Griffin's heart hammered. He'd had the perfect opening, the perfect chance to tell her the truth about Angela. But he hadn't been able to force the words from his mouth.

He pushed the thought of Angela to the back of his head. He'd arrived at Beth's house overwhelmed with the need to see her, hold her, smell her. Thoughts of Angela would only ruin the perfect elation he felt right now.

He slid his arms around Beth's back, over her firm butt, and down to her thighs. Heat flared as his tongue pushed deeper. He gripped her hips, his thumbs brushing beneath the fabric of her shirt and up to the silken skin on her stomach.

She traced his jawline with her fingertips. "You got me a tree."

Happiness overwhelmed him. Could she be more perfect?

He nuzzled her neck, his tongue exploring the curve of her earlobe. She shivered and tilted her head back, so he could trail kisses over the soft skin of her neck.

"Should I write you a cheesy song about how you should plant the tree in your yard as a symbol of how my love for you grows each day?" he murmured.

She gasped and his words bounced back, hitting him square in the chest.

Love. Fire spread through his veins. He'd loved people before, but the way he felt about Beth? His breath lodged in his throat. This was different. He'd never felt this before.

He grasped her tightly around the waist and buried his head in her hair. The scent of her flowery shampoo filled his senses, making him dizzy with need. "It's true. I'm crazy in love with you."

Her hands began to shake, and he pressed a kiss to the base of her wrist, where her pulse throbbed against his lips. His heart pounded in his chest. *Love me back. Need me like I need you.*

She caught his jaw in her hands and looked at him, her brown eyes filled with emotion. "I love you, too."

Four simple words, but they sucked all the air from his lungs. He clutched her, feeling the rise and fall of her chest against his.

They stood like that for a long time, their breaths mingling together as they basked in euphoria. Then she leaned up and kissed him, her soft lips caressing his and her firm breasts pressing into him.

Adrenaline rushed through his veins as desire consumed him. He lost himself in the taste of her mouth, the feel of her silken tongue against his.

She let out a small moan and dug her fingers into his back.

With his hands he traced her body, over the skin of her stomach, down her thighs, around to her butt. Her warm curves under his fingertips consumed every corner of his consciousness.

She arched against him, pressing herself into his hardness, heating his blood close to the point of boiling. He had to have her, all of her.

She unbuttoned his shirt and slid her hands inside, her palms soft and insistent on his bare chest.

He lifted her up, cupping her firm ass in his hands and strode across the living room. When he reached the sofa, he laid her down and leaned over her, bracing himself on his forearms.

She stared up at him, her eyes wide and her cheeks pink. The vulnerability on her face unleashed an aching need in him to be inside of her.

He took a long, shuddering breath. *First things first.*

With one hand, he yanked her shirt and released the clasp of her bra. Then he palmed her breast, her nipple a hard peak against his hand. He rolled his thumb over it, his penis throbbing as her nipple pebbled. He lowered his mouth and flicked his tongue across the surface of her nipple. She moaned and arched against him.

She reached down with both hands and quickly unzipped his pants and forced them down around his knees. He growled as her fingers closed around his penis, and he let himself rock into her hand. Once, then twice.

He grazed her nipple with his teeth, and she cried out, sending a sharp pain of need shooting through him.

Then she was arching off the sofa, practically climbing his body from feral need. He panted, his mind going fuzzy as he allowed her to push him into a sitting position and straddle his hips. Their warm breaths mingled together and a bead of sweat glistened on her forehead.

She wiggled her hips until her body cupped his erection. His head fell back as fireworks exploded inside his brain.

Holy shit. How much torture could one man take? He couldn't help himself. He had to be inside of her.

She lowered her hand to trace the hard ridges of his erection with her fingers. His cock jumped and he buried his head in her neck, grazing her skin with his teeth.

He lifted his hips from the sofa, deftly sliding out of his pants. Then he reached into his pocket and yanked out a condom.

He'd brought several, just in case.

* * *

She sucked in a breath as he slipped one finger inside to feel her wetness. She bucked against him, desire sending her body out of her control. He lifted a hand to touch her cheek but she turned her head and caught his thumb in her mouth. She ran her tongue along the bottom, sucking him into her mouth.

"Shit." His breath was ragged in her ear and his other hand wrapped around her hip bone.

Hunger unfurled inside of her and she thrust against him again, begging him to give her what she really needed.

With sure fingers he reached down and unfurled the condom over his length. She wrapped her fingers around him, smiling in satisfaction as he grew even harder in her hand.

He stared at her, a look of pure adoration and her heart throbbed in her chest. How had she never felt this before? How had nobody ever looked at her like that?

He threaded a hand in her hair, and she leaned into his touch, waves of emotion crashing over her.

He held her gaze as he gently entered her. She gripped his back, her fingers digging into his flesh as if she'd never let him go.

He moved deliberately, rocking into her. She matched his slow, steady rhythm, struggling to keep herself from moving harder and faster. She wanted every delicious second to last as long as possible.

Griffin gave a small shudder, and she knew he was doing the same, trying desperately to hold on and make it last.

Her muscles jerked as he found a spot she'd never known existed, making her body pulse with need.

"Oh," she gasped. She arched her back desperate to hold on to the sensation. His eyes traveled to her naked breasts and the heat in his expression made her tingle.

He used one hand to cup her ass and angle her closer. Stars exploded behind her eyes. His breathing grew faster, and she felt the muscles in his back tense and bunch under her fingers.

Her eyelids fluttered closed, and she lost herself in the sensation of his fingers on her skin, his hardness inside of her, stroking a place that made her body scream for delicious release.

Holy shit. She gritted her teeth and pushed away the curling tendrils of an orgasm. *Wait for him.*

Right before Griffin came, he would give a telltale tremor. She would wait until then to let go.

She lowered her mouth to his and took his bottom lip between hers, sucking gently, teasing. Heat rippled through her core. *Not yet.*

She buried her head in his neck and bit her lip, using all her willpower to keep the peak at bay. Griffin's arms wrapped around her and his strong fingers traced the notches of her spine. Something inside of her broke free and tore wide open.

She threw her head back and gave in, letting the orgasm overtake her. She was lost in sensation, him pulsing inside her and the needy bunching of her muscles as she tried to grip him. The heat went on and on, one never-ending wave of pleasure.

When her orgasm ebbed she went limp against him, melting into his body. His arms shuddered, and his neck twitched, but he continued to gently pump inside of her.

Beth lifted her head and traced his jaw with her fingers. His eyes were squeezed tight, his forehead furrowed.

Her eyes pricked with tears, and warmth washed over her. *God I love him.* His shaggy, blond hair, the stubble on his jaw, his strong arms around her, and his hands on her skin.

She pressed her forehead against his. "I freaking love you."

His eyes flew open and a wolfish grin crossed his face. "Yeah, you do."

Laughter bubbled out of her, but her amusement was interrupted by another wave of sensation. A delicious tingle built low in her belly and before she knew what was happening, she was writhing against him, moaning his name.

His jaw tightened, and he gave a small shudder.

"I love you." He whispered the words reverently, with his eyes locked on hers, his body bucking against hers.

They came together, clutching each other tightly.

When they'd both come down, he reclined against the sofa and she curled into his chest.

He brushed his lips over the top of her head. "I should really come over here more often."

CHAPTER SIXTEEN

He felt like one of those leaf-cutter ants that could carry fifty times its own body weight as he struggled to balance his ukulele, mandolin, and guitar case. He glanced at Beth, whose arms were loaded with reusable shopping bags. She'd also propped a cardboard box on her hip.

Yup. They were a pair of leaf-cutter ants.

"Have you thought any more about expanding your muffin business?"

He'd broached the subject with her last night, but she'd shut it down quickly with a reference to her bankruptcy.

She crinkled her nose. "I appreciate your faith in me, but I think you're overestimating the market for my muffins."

He snorted. Not possible. She delivered them three days a week and he was always sold out by 10:00 a.m.

She frowned as she unlocked the door to the theater. "To expand production I'd need a bigger, commercial kitchen. And to rent one of those, I'd have to take out a loan or get an investor. You know how much planning and risk goes into something like that. You've done well with Little Ray, but most people aren't that lucky."

He caught her gaze. "I know you could do it. And I'd help you if you wanted."

Her face paled. "I can't. I can't do it again. I don't want to do it again. I don't even know that I love muffins enough to make them my entire life."

His stomach twisted. That was all he needed to hear. If she didn't want to, then he'd drop the subject.

He leaned in to brush a kiss across her cheek. "Then I'm sorry I brought it up."

She sighed. "Thank you. I know you want me to be successful, but I like doing a lot of different things. I like that my days are never routine or boring and I'm always meeting new and interesting people and creating projects that only existed in my head."

He felt a small stab of guilt. Who was he to push Beth into a more traditional path? He liked that she did what made her happy and devoted her energy to creativity. It was part of what made her so damn amazing.

She hoisted the box higher into her arms. For the first time he could clearly read the marker scrawled across the side. It said, UNICORN HEADS.

He burst into laughter. "What on earth are you planning on doing with these kids?"

She wrenched the door open. "What do you mean?"

He stepped past her in the hallway, then propped the door open with his foot so she could slip through. "Unicorn heads?"

"Oh!" The corners of her mouth lifted. "Don't worry. They aren't *real* unicorn heads."

She sashayed past him, and he stood openmouthed, gaping after her.

Hands down, she was the weirdest, greatest person he'd ever known.

He climbed the stairs to the stage and began to unpack his instruments. Beth had asked him to perform a few songs, so the kids could play a game of freeze dance and of course he'd agreed. Now that Mandi worked at Little Ray full-time, he was finally able to have a life. She may have let the toilet overflow one night and she may have jammed the coffee grinder with one of her earrings, but the customers loved her.

A fully staffed Little Ray also meant he and Beth could go on real dates. Last week they'd even made it to a concert by one of Ryan's bands.

His chest swelled with satisfaction. Yeah, life was good. For the first time in a long time, he was completely happy.

"Daddy!" The sound of Mabel's footsteps echoed through the empty theater as she raced toward him.

She climbed onto the stage and threw herself into his arms. He lifted her up and spun her around. "Did you have a good day? Did you say thank you to Addie's mom for giving you a ride here?"

"Yup. Where's Beth?" She swiveled her head, searching the theater.

He chuckled as he set her down. At least he still got the first hug.

Beth stepped from backstage and bent, so Mabel could wrap her arms around her neck.

"Beth!" Mabel gave a sigh of satisfaction as she folded herself into Beth's embrace.

Beth lifted her into the air and squeezed her tight. "I missed you! Did you have a good day?"

His heart hammered. When he saw the two of them together, it brought the world sharply into focus.

"Hello, hello!" a woman's voice called. He tore his gaze from May and Beth to see Addie and her mom, Gwen, climbing the stairs to the stage.

He lifted a hand in greeting. "Hey, Gwen. Thanks so much for giving Mabel a ride. It gave us a little extra time to set things up."

"No problem!"

The number of names on Mabel's approved emergency contacts at school was quickly growing. Just last week he'd added Beth and Gwen. If it really took a village to raise a child, he was finally assembling Mabel's village.

Addie ran to Beth's side and grabbed her hand. "Did you bring the new costumes? Can we see them?"

"Of course. They're back here. But remember, you only get to pick one. Everyone else needs a costume, too." She led both girls behind the thick red curtain.

Gwen joined him. "What do you think about letting the girls have a sleepover? Maybe next weekend? Addie's been begging me to have Mabel stay the night."

His gut clenched, and he nearly dropped the ukulele in his hand. "A sleepover?"

She was only four. Was she really old enough to have a sleepover? Every night for the last four years, he'd pressed a kiss to her forehead before he went to bed. They'd never spent a night away from each other.

She paused. "Well, yes. I think the girls would have fun, don't you?"

He swallowed hard against the rising panic. Of course she'd have fun. But what if she got homesick or had a bad dream or needed a drink of water in the middle of the night?

"I need to think about it."

And he needed to talk to Beth. Was it unreasonable to be so worried? After all, it was just a sleepover. Beth would tell him if he was being overprotective.

Gwen gave a small nod of understanding. "It sucks, doesn't it? Them growing up? Sometimes I feel like time is racing past me and before I know it she'll be in college and moving out of the house."

His stomach dropped. He didn't want to think about that for a very long time.

"Am I that obvious?" He also didn't want to be that dad, the one who never let his kid do anything.

She laughed. "Trust me, we all feel the same way."

"Beth and I will talk about it, and I'll let you know." His gaze automatically went to Beth. She stood on the other end of the stage, helping the girls wriggle into costumes. His heart squeezed. She'd help him make the right decision for Mabel.

Gwen followed his gaze and smiled. "Mabel is always welcome. You just let me know. And Griffin?"

He looked at her.

"I'm glad you met someone. Well, not just someone, but Beth. Being alone is hard, and she's especially fantastic."

"Yeah. She is." It was a fact that only became clearer with each passing day.

Loud voices echoed as another group of kids entered the theater.

"I guess I'd better grab a seat for rehearsal," Gwen said, stepping toward the stairs that led from the stage to the auditorium.

"Thanks again for bringing Mabel."

His attention quickly shifted back to Beth and Mabel, who was now singing and twirling in a circle. Beth reached out and tucked a stray clump of hair back into May's princess hat.

His chest grew tight. Beth was fantastic, but there was still one thing holding him back. Sooner or later he had to tell her the truth about Angela. He couldn't keep dragging it out. But how? Trepidation filled him. How the hell was he supposed to tell Beth that Mabel had been an accident? That Angela was a groupie and a drug addict and the whole relationship had been a mistake?

Pain ripped through him. It would change the way she saw him. How could it not? And he wanted to shove all of that into the past and forget it had ever happened. It was why he'd moved to Belmont in the first place.

His life was finally what he'd hoped for, which was why he had to get it all out there. Beth deserved the truth. And she would understand. She had to.

* * *

Mabel skipped ahead of them on the sidewalk to Beth's house. When she reached the front door, she hopped from side to side, from one foot to the other.

"Are you sure Black Kitty is a boy? What if the cat doctor was wrong? Can you ask him to check again?"

Beth chuckled to herself as she twisted her key in the lock. "The veterinarian is very sure that Black Kitty is a boy. Sorry, Mabel."

She'd been meaning to talk to Griffin about that. Mabel loved Black Kitty, but she'd been crushed when they'd discovered he was a boy. Plus, he'd started attacking Beth's feet at night. Maybe Black Kitty needed a sister.

As soon as she cracked the door, Mabel burst into the house. "Oh, Black Kitty, I'm here! It's me, Mabel, your best friend in the whole world. Where are you?"

Griffin raised an eyebrow. Beth laughed and stepped over the threshold.

Mabel stood in the middle of the living room with Black Kitty clutched tightly to her chest. She was singing "It's Raining Men" to him. Where on earth had she learned that song?

Beth shook her head and turned in the direction of the kitchen. As far as songs went, it was pretty harmless. Besides, it was nearly seven and Mabel got cranky if she wasn't in bed by eight thirty. They didn't have time to worry about Mabel's musical selections right now.

Griffin followed her into the kitchen. "Ryan made her another mix CD."

She chuckled as she grabbed the cutting board. He opened

the refrigerator and pulled out a bunch of kale and some chicken.

He set them on the counter next to her and cleared his throat. "So, Gwen asked if Mabel wanted to have a sleepover with Addie next week."

"Oh yeah?" She'd noticed that Mabel and Addie were quickly becoming best friends.

"Yeah." He scrubbed a hand over his face. "I don't know. Do you think it's a good idea?"

The back of her neck prickled. "Me?"

He lifted his eyes to meet hers. "Yeah, you. You know kids better than I do. Do you think Mabel's old enough for a sleepover?"

She turned to the cutting board and focused on slicing the kale. "What do you think?"

He stepped behind her, his breath warm on the back of her neck, and wrapped a hand around her waist. "I don't know. I want to know what you think. I want your opinion."

His mouth was inches from her neck and she flushed, her body growing warm.

"Um." She sighed and turned to face him, meeting his gaze.

Her throat was tight. This was why she'd told him she'd never try to replace Mabel's mom. That was a line she had to be careful not to cross, for all of their sakes. But he was asking for her opinion. Which meant she should give it. Right?

She took a deep breath. "I think it would be good for her. And I think she'd have fun. But if she doesn't, she can just call us and we can go get her."

He frowned. "You don't think that would embarrass her? Or scare her? What if she goes and she doesn't have a good time and then she's too afraid to go on another one?"

She raised onto her tiptoes and pressed the tip of her nose to his. "Mabel? Embarrassed? Have you met your daughter? The other night at Little Ray she told everyone she was going to marry a hippo when she grew up."

He laughed, and the tension in her neck eased. "I think you're a worrier and that's part of what makes you a good dad. I also think she's your baby and it's hard to see her grow up, but you can't protect her from everything. We'll be here, ready to catch her if she falls. I think the best thing you can do is let her try. If she fails you'll help her through it."

She held her breath, her heart pounding. *I'm not trying to be her.* She hoped he knew that, hoped he understood.

Sometimes she wanted to force him to address it and make him tell her about Angela. What she'd been like or what she'd wanted for May or anything really. At least then she wouldn't have to grapple with the anxiety of not knowing and the possibility that she'd unwittingly say or do something that stirred up painful memories.

But most of the time things were so perfect between them that she didn't worry. Griffin would confide in her when he was ready.

He dropped a kiss onto her lips. "I think you have me pegged. And I think you're completely right."

She nuzzled into his neck. "I like it when you say that."

He pressed himself closer and lowered his mouth to nibble her ear.

A flash of heat rushed through her and she closed her eyes, losing herself in the haze of his coffee scent.

"Daddy?"

Griffin jumped back.

Mabel stood in the doorway, Black Kitty still dangling from her arms. "What are you guys doing?"

Beth spun back to the cutting board and resumed chopping. This was for him to handle.

"Oh, um…" Griffin paused. "We were just talking about a sleepover. For you. At Addie's house. Would you like to have a sleepover?"

The shriek she emitted was deafening. Beth heard the scrabbling of kitty claws on the tile and assumed Black Kitty had hightailed it to a quieter location.

"Daddy! I can go on a sleepover? Like a big girl? When? Can I go tomorrow? Can we dress like princesses and eat cookies and watch movies and stay up late and sleep on the floaty bed?"

Beth had to give it to him, Griffin deserved an A when it came to distraction techniques for four-year-olds.

"The floaty bed?" he asked.

"You know. With the air. Like in the pool. And you put your mouth on it and puff, puff, puff, then magic. It's a real bed."

There was a long silence.

Beth pushed the kale to one side and picked up the package of chicken. "She means an air mattress. I have one Mabel. You can borrow it. But we need to ask Addie's mommy because she might have a really nice sofa for you, or you might even be able to sleep in the same bed."

Another earsplitting squeal.

Yup, Mabel was ready to have a sleepover.

CHAPTER SEVENTEEN

Beth leaned forward in the passenger seat and scanned the side of the road for street signs. Ryan had said the outdoor venue was a hard-left turn thirty minutes outside of Belmont, which meant they should see it any moment. Next to her Griffin hummed something she didn't recognize with the occasional "ba ba bow" she'd learned indicated guitar strumming.

She spotted it, the green sign lettered GILCREST DR. "There it is. Make a left."

As he turned, sloshing and clinking emanated from the backseat. She twisted to examine the twenty or so mason jars she'd managed to cram into the car, along with the five boxes of mini-muffins. Her mission for the day was to prove that people loved pickles as much as they loved baked goods.

Griffin grimaced. "Is everything all right back there? I don't want the car to smell like vinegar for the next year."

She narrowed her eyes at him. "They're all fine. I told you, I followed the directions for sealing the jars exactly."

Her garden was out of control and she could hide only so many vegetables under cheese sauce before Mabel caught on. So Beth had started canning. Now they had enough jars to get them through several months of a zombie apocalypse.

He raised an eyebrow at her. "When you said you were pickling everything I didn't know you meant you were literally pickling *everything*."

She chuckled. Sometimes he was no better than his daughter. He'd been willing to sample the pickled carrots, beets, and okra, but he'd drawn the line at pumpkin.

"Complain all you like. I bet my pickled everything will be a huge hit."

He covered her hand with his and squeezed. "You're right. I bet the cauliflower disappears before anyone so much as looks at your muffins."

He sounded like Ryan, who'd mumbled something about her pickles and the "unsuspecting public." Not that she put much stock in Ryan's culinary preferences. The man ate microwavable noodles every night for dinner.

She scrunched her nose. "Very funny. I'll take that bet. What should we wager?"

He slanted her a look, and his pupils dilated.

Blood pounded in her ears. It was Mabel's first sleepover. After Ryan's show they would have the entire night to themselves.

She placed her hand on his leg and inched her fingers up his thigh. "Great minds think alike."

He let out a low growl. "We're almost there. If you torture me now, I'll have to take my revenge later."

Goose bumps broke out over her skin. *Yes, please.*

"Mmmm, pickles." She licked her lips.

He made a choking sound. "You did not go there."

She waggled an eyebrow. "I did. And I know that if I opened one of those jars right now and showed you just how much I love to lick pickles, you'd turn this car around immediately."

He jerked the car onto the shoulder and came to an abrupt stop. He shifted into park at the same time he unbuckled his seat belt.

Half a second later, his mouth was on hers.

She tilted her head back and closed her eyes, relishing the feel of his lips and his caramel-coffee scent.

His tongue dipped into her mouth and her heart raced.

Abruptly, he pulled back and sat in his seat, a self-satisfied smirk on his lips.

She blinked at him. "That's it?"

He leaned over and traced a hand down her collarbone, skimming inside the top of her bra.

Her breath quickened and a pulsing need built between her legs.

But the moment she arched into his touch, he snatched his hand back.

She unhooked her seat belt, grabbed his hand and tugged it back in her direction. He watched as she placed his palm over her breast.

His jaw worked and his eyes stayed glued to her chest.

She leaned across the center console, but before she reached him his phone started to ring.

Shit. She flopped back into her seat. He had to take it. What if Mabel needed something at the sleepover?

He growled and reached for his phone.

"It's Ryan." Griffin's eyes flashed, but he still lifted the phone to his ear. "What?"

She could hear the hum of a voice on the other end, but couldn't make out the words.

With a huff, Griffin buckled his seat belt. When she did the same, he shifted the car back into Drive. "Yeah. We'll be there in three minutes."

He hung up the phone and dropped it into the center console.

"Well, we both lose. Now I *do* want to turn around and take you straight home, but Ryan says there's some kind of band emergency, and he needs me there immediately."

She loosened her seat belt enough to lean over and nibble his earlobe. "I can wait. I have you all to myself all night long."

Her spine tingled. It would be the first time they'd spent the night together.

He trailed one hand over her bare arm, making her shiver. "Trust me. I plan to make good use of it. I'm just not very patient."

They rounded another bend in the road and came upon a cluster of wooden picnic tables. And a handful of people.

She heaved a sigh and slumped back into the seat. *Later.*

Griffin pulled into the gravel lot and parked. A short distance away, there was a stage where guys were plugging amps into guitars and setting up the drums.

They barely had time to park before Ryan came loping toward them. They stepped out of the car, and Griffin walked to her side. He threaded his hand with hers, leaned close, and whispered in her ear. "Don't let me forget that I promised to torture you later. I'm looking forward to my payback."

Anticipation rose inside of her. That sounded promising.

Ryan came to a halt in front of them, his face flushed and his breathing ragged.

"Thank God you're here. The idiot guitar player broke his hand. We're expecting over a hundred people, including a few scouts for all the local venues. We were counting on tonight to get them the gigs they need to sell this CD. They need to get their name out there, starting immediately."

Ryan leaned toward Griffin and clapped a hand on his shoulder. "We need you. I'd never normally ask you this, but we need someone to fill in for him."

Griffin's eyebrows shot up. "Me?"

Ryan's jaw set. "Yes, you. I've heard Thorny Lemon and I know you can play. You've heard their CD, I gave it to you the other week. You can pick up enough of the songs to fake your way through a set." Ryan sighed and scrubbed a hand over his chin. "Please, man. I'm desperate and you're the only person I can think of who won't fuck this up completely."

That was one way to ask nicely.

Griffin turned to her, his eyes dark and his forehead furrowed.

She squeezed his hand. "Do you want to?"

She'd seen the way his face lit up when he talked about performing with Thorny Lemon.

He gave a tight nod.

She shrugged. "Then why not? You'll have fun."

His eyes lightened. He squared his shoulders and turned to Ryan. "Okay. I'll do it. But I can't promise any fantastic, earth-shattering performance. I only have, what, an hour to learn the songs?"

Ryan nodded eagerly. "Yeah, but you'll be better than that asshole with the broken hand."

He pointed in the direction of the stage. "Let's go then. I have a guitar for you. You'll want to meet the rest of the group, get the crib sheets, and have time to run through the songs a few times."

Griffin glanced at her. "You're sure you don't mind?"

Warmth washed over her. As if he had to ask.

"Of course I don't mind. Go. Have fun!" She gave him a slight push. "And don't be afraid to show off a little."

She'd seen him in his music room and she knew what he was capable of. He was the sexiest man she'd ever seen with a guitar. Even hotter than Dave Navarro or old-school Jon Bon Jovi.

Griffin bent to kiss her on the cheek and then trotted away with Ryan, like a puppy with a bone. She grinned at his retreating back. Just wait until she got her hands on him tonight.

Her phone pinged and she pulled it out of her purse.

A group text message.

> Kate: This thing starts at six thirty, right? Beth, are you already there?
>
> Beth: Yup.
>
> Beth: Don't worry, even if the muffins go fast, I still have lots of pickles.

Ainsley sent a smiling poop emoticon.

Beth: I used all organic vegetables. Pumpkin makes your hair glossy, carrots make your nails strong, and broccoli can help you lose weight.

She'd tried the first two factoids on Mabel, with no success.

Ainsley: You pickled broccoli?!?!?!?!

Kate: I don't know how I feel about this...

What was it with all the pickle haters?

Kate: James says if we aren't careful, Beth's going to start sneaking pickles into the muffins.

Ainsley sent another poop emoticon.

Beth's mind began to whir. Pickle muffins. It wasn't a bad idea.

* * *

Griffin strummed a chord on the unfamiliar guitar. Under his fingers, the strings vibrated, and the sound resonated through the speakers on either side of the stage.

His pulse sped as the notes thrummed through his body. Perfection. There was nothing like standing on a stage, sharing sound with real, live people.

He met Beth's eyes in the crowd and his adrenaline surged. Almost nothing.

He squeezed his eyes closed and let the notes wash over him.

He should be nervous. He'd never met the band members or played their songs before today. Hell, he hardly even listened to folk music. But now that he was onstage, surrounded by the music, pure determination flooded his veins.

He opened his eyes and stood a little straighter, pushing his shoulders back. Screw the crib notes he'd taped to the stage floor. He was a musician. Music was in his soul, and performing always transported him.

Pride and elation filled him as he allowed his gaze to travel out over the crowd. Two hundred people, if he had to guess. Not bad for an album debut by a brand-new band.

The drummer broke into a polyrhythm and he followed, lowering his head to watch his fingers on the strings. He nearly missed the intro note for his guitar solo, but quickly recovered from his mistake. He swayed as he played, the music flowing through every muscle and fiber in his body.

There was something about performing for an audience that had always made him feel as if he were on top of the world. He hadn't played for a crowd in years. It was exhilarating. Intoxicating. By the time they hit the song's last note, he was sweaty and flushed with euphoria.

Thunderous applause rippled through the crowd, forcing him to lift his head.

He panted as the group came into focus before his eyes. His face stretched in a broad grin that threatened to split him open.

The drummer clicked his sticks in the air three times before they launched into another song.

This time, Griffin tried to keep his eyes on the crowd. He watched Beth and Kate, shimmying and gyrating together; Ainsley, who'd angled her back to the two of them as if they were strangers; Ryan who stood next to the stage, arms crossed over his chest, tapping his feet in time and grinning like a maniac.

Griffin's fingers danced across the strings as if this music, with its twanging guitar and the heart-wrenching melodies, were his. The notes and lyrics flowed from him as naturally as if he'd written them himself. He relaxed his stance and gave himself over to the music.

The sound of his younger years had been dark and angsty, full of frantic rhythms and grating vocals. Back then, it had resonated with him. So, what did this sound, the nostalgic unself-conscious music he was playing, say about him now?

The question flickered in his head, but before he had time to figure it out, the set was over. As the last notes floated through the air he held his guitar high and let the swell of the crowd buoy him. He was sweaty and flushed, but triumphant and ecstatic. His first live show since... He froze. His first live show since Mabel was born.

With a shake of the head, he hopped off the stage. It had been good to feel that heady excitement again, even if it was just for tonight. It was addictive, but he couldn't let himself get sucked in. He had a family and a business to consider.

Beth raced toward him and he scooped her into his arms, kissing her hard on the mouth. When he released her, she glowed up at him, her eyes filled with adoration.

"You were amazing."

Ryan bounded over and jostled him into a bear hug. "I knew it! You're the best, man, the best. You did even better than the regular guitarist. I've already had three requests for shows. You have to start practicing with them, you have to keep this going. This has the potential to be something pretty awesome."

Griffin's gut twisted. He couldn't. Rehearsals and shows meant time away from Mabel. She was the reason he'd gotten out of the music business in the first place.

Beth gently squeezed his elbow and lifted onto her tiptoes to whisper in his ear. "We can make it work. Sarah and Mandi and Brian and Cora will help you with Little Ray, and it'll give me a chance to have one-on-one time with May. That is, if you want to."

His chest swelled. She was right. This wasn't Shepherdsville. He and Mabel had built a community in Belmont. They had friends. And they had Beth.

A lump formed in his throat. He could be a musician again. A real one.

"I can help with Mabel, too. Like watch her sometimes," Ryan offered.

He choked back a laugh. He appreciated the thought, but he wasn't so sure Ryan would make a good babysitter. After all, he had been the one to introduce May to a song about cannibals. And he did like to put fake bugs in people's cups.

Ryan grinned back at him, his blue eyes bright with expectation.

To his surprise, he felt himself relenting. Why not? Ryan would definitely keep her entertained. And more than most people, he could probably match her boundless energy.

"I'm not sure you want to do that to yourself. Mabel can be challenging."

Ryan laughed. "Then we should get along well. Did I ever tell you about the time when I was seven and I climbed onto the roof?"

Beth's eyebrows nearly shot off her forehead. "You know that recounting all the ways you nearly died as a child isn't going to convince us to let you babysit Mabel, right? We'd like her back alive."

"Well then what about if I get Kate or Ainsley to help out? You know, until I get the hang of things. How hard can it be to take care of a kid for a few hours?"

Griffin looped an arm around his friend's shoulder. How could he say no, when Ryan so clearly wanted to help? Besides, Ryan had a good heart. There were worse people Mabel could learn from.

"In addition to keeping her off the roof, you should probably keep her sober. And all in one piece. Oh, and if you could keep her from burning down the house or flooding the house or driving my car into a pole, those would all be good, too."

Ryan pretended to frown. "Well, now that I know all of that is involved…"

Beth elbowed him. "I'm sure you can manage it. But for now, let's get a beer, okay?"

Griffin threaded an arm around her waist and pulled her close. A beer sounded good. But then he had to get her home. He had a busy night planned.

CHAPTER EIGHTEEN

Griffin sagged into his office chair and took a large gulp of coffee. He'd been up late last night, practicing with his new band. And when he got home, he'd found Beth and Mabel passed out in May's twin-size bed.

His heart thudded as he recalled the sight of Mabel curled onto Beth's chest and Beth with one arm wrapped protectively around her. Several loose pages of the children's book they'd written and illustrated had been strewn around them.

Sarah flew into his office, her purple hair sticking out in every direction. "Brian just puked in the bathroom. I'm sending him home, and I need you to come out front and help fill orders."

He jumped from the chair. "Is he okay? You think it's contagious?"

She made a gagging noise. "I hope not. At least he made it to the bathroom. You don't pay me enough to clean up puke, but I did. I even sprayed a little air freshener around, so we should be good."

He groaned as he followed her through the doorway. Puke wasn't good for business.

He strode past the line of customers waiting at the counter and poked his head into the bathroom.

Orange scent assaulted his nostrils and lungs, making him cough. He glanced quickly around the room. No visible puke and no puke smell. Fogging the room with air freshener wasn't how he would have handled it, but it was too late now.

He jogged over to the counter and took his place in front of the milk steamer.

An hour later, the constant influx of orders had just started to slow when Sarah tapped him on the shoulder.

She jerked her chin toward a man in a suit, who stood in front of the pastry-display case. "This guy wants to talk to you about the muffins."

He forced a smile and stepped from behind the counter. No doubt the guy wanted to place a large order, or reserve a dozen. Both of which were impossible unless Beth decided to expand production, and she'd already made her feelings on that clear.

He held out a hand. "Griffin Hall."

The short, stocky man shook it. "Fred Gallantry."

His mind reeled. Fred Gallantry? He owned a well-known restaurant chain in the city.

"Mr. Gallantry." Griffin showed him to a small, two-person table in the corner. Griffin took the seat with his back against the wall, so he could keep an eye on the rest of the shop.

"You can call me Fred. Quite an operation you have here."

Griffin nodded politely. He doubted Mr. Gallantry had much interest in Little Ray. He liked his restaurants large, swanky, and overpriced.

"Sarah said you wanted to ask about the muffins?" Better get to the heart of the matter, so he could get back to work.

Gallantry's lips thinned as he pressed them together. "Yes. Neither of us has time to waste, do we? I heard your girlfriend is the one who makes your muffins. As you may know, I'm about to open a grocery store in town and I thought she and I could reach a business arrangement."

The line of customers was growing again and his anxiety began to build. He didn't have long to talk. "I'll let her know you came by, but I don't think she's interested in expanding."

Gallantry frowned and rubbed his chin. "How do you know she isn't interested when you haven't heard my offer?"

Griffin sighed and slumped back against the chair. Fine. He'd hear the guy out.

Gallantry pressed the tips of his index fingers together, creating a steeple.

"I want to buy one-third of her business. She'd retain the controlling shares. In return, she would regularize her methods, expand production, hire more employees, and find a fully outfitted commercial kitchen. She would provide my new high-end grocery store with all of its muffin requirements and," he waved a hand, indicating Little Ray's dining room, "she could sell the rest at places like this."

Griffin drummed his fingers on the table. He doubted Beth was interested, but it should be her decision.

Gallantry stared him down. "And you of all people

should know that one hundred thousand dollars is a very fair price."

Griffin fell into a coughing fit. One hundred thousand dollars? The man had to be joking.

Gallantry smirked. "I trust you'll relate the offer to her?"

"If you leave a card with me, I'll be happy to tell her exactly what you told me and ask her to get in touch."

He doubted she'd be as excited as Gallantry seemed to expect, but it was her decision. Beth wasn't the corporate-business type. She wasn't just scared of another bankruptcy, although he knew that was a factor. She liked her freedom, liked being able to create when the mood struck her. She enjoyed baking, and it made her a decent living, but she seemed reluctant to dedicate all of her time and energy to it. And they both knew that's what being a small-business owner required.

His gaze flicked back to the line forming by the counter.

"I'm sorry, but I have to get back to work. It was nice to meet you." Griffin held out his hand.

Gallantry shook it. "Please be sure to tell her about my proposal. As soon as possible." Then he turned and headed for the door.

Griffin's stomach clenched. Of course he'd tell her about Gallantry's offer. But the guy had no idea of the type of person he was dealing with. Beth wasn't motivated by money or recognition, and it was one of the things Griffin loved most about her.

In the end, she'd do whatever she felt was best for her.

* * *

Griffin's name flashed across Beth's phone. She took her foot off the pedal for the sewing machine and snatched up the phone. He was supposed to meet her at her place in thirty minutes. For…lunch.

"I'm so sorry, Beth. I have to cancel. Matt got sick, so I sent him home. I have to work the counter for a few hours."

She bit back her disappointment. "Is he okay?"

"I'm sure he'll be fine. He probably has a bug or ate some bad sushi." There was a long pause.

"There's something else I have to tell you." His tone turned serious, making the nape of her neck prickle.

He exhaled loudly. "Fred Gallantry, the guy with all the restaurants in the city? He came by to talk to me. He wants me to tell you that he's offering to buy a one-third share of the muffin business for one hundred thousand dollars."

She nearly fell out of her chair.

"One hundred thousand dollars?" she squeaked.

He gave a slow, rumbling laugh. "Yup. One hundred thousand dollars. You'd retain controlling shares."

A funny feeling built in the pit of her stomach. "So what does he want?"

He sighed. She'd known there was a catch.

"He wants you to expand. Hire employees. Get a commercial kitchen. Commit to providing his new grocery store with all the muffins they need."

Suddenly her mouth tasted sour. Fred Gallantry wanted her to launch a full-fledged business. He wanted her to commit all of her time and energy to muffins. Which meant no more sewing and no more children's theater. That's how running a full-time business worked.

If it failed? She'd lose everything again, just like the first time. And she wasn't sure that muffins were her true passion. What if her life's work was supposed to be a mixture of part-time projects and creations? After all, that made her a lot happier than she'd been when she was trying to juggle the day-to-day demands of running her business. It was the creating she really cared about.

Griffin was silent on the other end of the phone.

She took a ragged breath. "That's a lot to think about."

"You don't have to do it. Just because it's a good financial offer doesn't mean you should do it."

His voice was warm and soothing.

Her mind spun. It was a great offer. A hundred thousand dollars and the chance to run her own business again. So why did she feel like she was about to puke?

She chewed a fingernail. "I don't know that I want muffins to be my whole life."

Griffin gave a low chuckle. "I *know* I don't want muffins to be your whole life."

A smile tugged at the corners of her mouth and she closed her eyes, willing her thoughts to crystallize.

It took only a second.

"I just don't know that I love muffins that much. Do I love them more than children's theater and sewing and making costumes and...?" She trailed off. She didn't make money doing all of those things, but they mattered. To her, at least.

She swallowed. "Does that make me crazy?"

"No." His voice was firm and decisive. "You're far from crazy. I think you'd be crazy to take the offer and commit everything to a business you're not completely passionate about."

Exactly. Relief flooded her and she sank back against her chair. She wasn't ready to turn muffins into her entire life.

There was a blink of silence on the other end of the line, signaling that he had an incoming call.

He cursed under his breath. "Beth, can you hang on one second? Mabel's school is on the other line. If she's 'making it rain' confetti during nap time again, she's going to be in a lot of trouble."

Beth swallowed her giggle. It had been hard to keep a straight face while enforcing that time-out when Mabel got home.

"Yeah, of course."

A minute later Griffin beeped back onto the line.

"She's sick. Says her tummy hurts. Her fever is a hundred and one. They want me to come and get her, but it's going to be another few hours before I can get anyone else in for the closing shift."

She jumped from her chair and grabbed the keys on their hook by the door. At the jingling sound, Black Kitty crouched low and wiggled his butt in the air.

"I'll go get her." She dodged past Black Kitty and slipped out the front door.

"That would be a lifesaver, thank you."

She unlocked Martha's driver's-side door. "I'm more than

happy to accept that thank-you in the form of pho. I'll call you in a few and let you know how she's doing."

"You know I love you, right?" His voice was low and intense.

A ripple of satisfaction spread through her.

"I love you, too. And I'll see you tonight." She hung up the phone and drove in the direction of Mabel's school.

She pulled Martha into a spot near the front and hustled to the door. Once inside she made a beeline for the front office. The nurse's office had to be close to it, right?

"Beth!" The little wail echoed through the empty hallway. Beth backed up a step and peered into the closest room.

Mabel stood in front of a white cot, her pink sneakers in a pool of vomit.

Beth swallowed the bile that rose in her throat. *It's just a little puke.*

Fat tears rolled down Mabel's cheeks as she held her arms out in the air. Her chin wobbled. "I needed you."

It was enough to gut her. She rushed to Mabel and scooped her into her arms, clutching her little body close.

"I know baby. I'm so sorry." She had to remind herself to breathe through her mouth, not her nose.

The nurse stared at them, her mouth hanging open.

It's just a little puke.

It seemed that was destined to be her mantra for the day. She could recite it to herself as she did the loads of laundry that loomed in her future.

Then the nurse's mouth curled into a smile. "I take it you're Beth?"

She nodded.

"Mabel's been asking for you. And her daddy. And Black Kitty."

She smiled. "Black Kitty is her cat."

That had become more than clear over the last few weeks. Beth might be Black Kitty's keeper, but his loyalty and love lay entirely with Mabel.

Mabel grabbed a fistful of Beth's hair and buried her head into Beth's shoulder.

"I missed you," she whispered.

Beth clutched her tighter and kissed the top of her head. "I missed you, too. Are you ready to go home?"

"Yes." Mabel's voice was uncharacteristically soft. They'd tried, in vain, to teach her the difference between an indoor voice and an outdoor voice. Apparently it took the flu to make the lesson stick.

Beth bent, still holding Mabel in her arms, to pick up the pink backpack from the floor. "What was her temperature?"

"One hundred and one. We're not allowed to medicate them. Legal reasons."

Beth resisted the urge to roll her eyes. They really couldn't give May some medicine to get her fever down?

She pressed the back of her hand to Mabel's forehead, as her mom had done for her. May was burning up.

"Do you want to eat a popsicle and watch some TV when we get home?"

"No," Mabel groaned.

She frowned. Declining sugar and TV? Mabel was definitely sick.

She retraced her steps out of the school and into the parking lot, where she trudged toward Martha.

When she opened the rear passenger door, Mabel clutched her tighter "Don't put me down! I don't want you to put me down!"

The words hit her like a punch to the gut.

She lowered her head and pressed her cheek to Mabel's feverish forehead. "I love you sweet girl. I'm here now, and I'm going to take you home, and we're going to have a snuggly girls' day."

Mabel stilled in her arms. "You promise? You won't leave me?"

Her heart twisted painfully. "I would never leave you. But first I have to strap you into the car so we can go home. This doesn't seem like a fun place to have girls' day, does it?"

Mabel shook her flushed face from side to side. She allowed Beth to settle her into the car seat and buckle the seat belt across her chest.

Then she stuck a thumb in her mouth and pointed at Beth. "I'm sorry."

Beth followed May's finger, glancing down the front of her shirt. Which was streaked with puke.

It's just a little vomit. She shrugged, then slammed the passenger door shut and climbed into the driver's seat.

The only thing that mattered was getting Mabel home.

CHAPTER NINETEEN

Beth stepped out of the shower and toweled her short hair. Mabel had fallen fast asleep in the car and hadn't even woken up when Beth had carried her into the house, wiped her down with a washcloth, and slipped her into her pajamas.

Beth wished she could sleep like that. It was a gift.

She padded into the bedroom and opened the door to Griffin's closet. She selected a soft, flannel, button-down shirt from a hanger and stepped into it. The sleeves fell over her hands, so she rolled them up. Then she buried her nose in the collar and inhaled his coffee scent.

The chime of the doorbell made her jump.

She stepped into the hall and peered down the stairs and through the glass window above the door. From this angle she could make out a woman with blond hair. Not Ainsley, whose hair was a more golden color. This woman had hair so blond it was almost white.

Beth descended the stairs and peeked through the peephole. The woman was thin, with pale skin to go with the light-blond hair. Beth's spine tingled. There was something familiar about her. They'd probably met before, at Little Ray or a show for one of Ryan's bands.

Well, she couldn't just leave one of Griffin's friends standing on the doorstep. And his shirt covered as much of her as most of her dresses did.

She unlocked the door and cracked it open wide enough to poke her head out.

"Hi." The woman bit her lip.

Beth smiled at her. "Hi! What can I help you with?"

The woman glanced at the numbers on the house. "Is Griffin here?"

Beth shook her head. "No, sorry. He's at work. Do you want me to call and tell him you're here, or would you rather stop by there?"

The woman's brown eyes fixed her, and she felt another wisp of familiarity. Where did she know her from?

Usually she was good at remembering names.

The woman gripped her worn, leather purse with both hands. "I'm Angela."

The world spun in front of Beth's eyes, and panic threaded through her lungs, making it impossible to breathe. She gripped the door frame and struggled to suck in a breath. Then another.

Angela?

Griffin's Angela?

Mabel's mother, Angela?

Her knees wobbled and it took all her effort to remain upright. Of course the woman looked familiar. Traces of Mabel were etched in all of her features.

Angela's eyes brimmed with tears. "From your reaction, I'm guessing you know who I am?"

Beth gulped in another breath and steadied herself. "I know you're Mabel's mom if that's what you're asking."

"Can I see her?" Angela's eyes were pleading, her voice little more than a whisper.

Her stomach twisted and her fingers curled around the rolled cuffs of Griffin's shirtsleeves.

Guilt mixed with shock and pain. She couldn't let this woman in to see Mabel, even if she was her mom. Griffin had to have a reason for lying about Angela.

"She's sick. She's been throwing up, she has a fever and she just fell asleep. I don't think she's up for any kind of company."

Angela nodded, her throat working. "Oh. Okay. Will you have Griffin call me when he gets back? Tell him I want to see her."

Panic coursed through Beth's veins. Angela was alive. Angela wanted to see Mabel. Beth struggled to wrap her head around it. Why had he lied to her? What did it mean? For all of them?

"This is my number." Angela handed her a small scrap of paper. Beth's fingers closed around it, crushing it into her palm.

Then, her heart lodged firmly in her throat, she watched as Angela walked to a dark sedan that was parked next to Martha.

What the hell was going on?

Griffin had a lot of explaining to do.

* * *

He climbed the front stairs two at a time and unlocked the door with one swift turn of the key. It had been a long day, but he was finally home. Home to Beth and Mabel.

He found Beth standing in the hall, wearing one of his button-down shirts. The sleeves were rolled to her elbows, and the shirttails hit her mid-thigh. Heat raced through him as he brushed a kiss over her temple. Her body was stiff against him.

"Nice outfit."

She stepped away, her mouth compressed into a thin line. His spine prickled. What was wrong?

"May puked on me, so I had to borrow your shirt. Well, she puked on herself, but she was crying and wanted to be picked up, so I wound up with puke all over me."

He glanced up the stairs in the direction of the bedrooms. "Is she okay?"

"She's fine." Beth's lips remained pinched and her expression tight.

"Then what's wrong?" It wasn't like Beth to get angry over a little puke.

He rubbed his hands over her arms and studied her face. Her expression was flat, her eyes dull, and the skin around her mouth stretched with worry. Normally she'd make a joke about the shirt and the puke. Something else was on her mind. Something serious.

She pulled away and shifted her gaze to the floor, tears building in her eyes. "Angela came by today." Beth's voice was barely louder than a whisper.

Shards of glass slid down his spine, and fear clenched in his stomach.

"Angela?"

Beth took another step back and crossed her arms across her chest. The pain in her eyes ripped him apart.

"She wanted to see Mabel."

Bile rose in his throat. "Please tell me you didn't let her."

Her eyes flashed with anger. "Of course I didn't let her see Mabel! I figured there was a reason you let me think she was dead."

Fear lurched through him. He reached for her again, but she stepped back and bumped into the wall.

"Please don't touch me right now."

A pain shot through his rib cage.

He sucked in a long breath and steeled himself. "She signed over all her parental rights three years ago and we haven't seen or heard from her since. I thought..."

He stepped toward Beth slowly, his palms upturned. Of course she was angry. He'd lied to her, when he should have told her everything. Fuck. He'd wanted so badly for Angela to be out of their lives forever. He'd wanted to pretend they could move on and be a normal, happy family, without her shadow looming over them.

"I thought she was still in jail. Or maybe dead. She's a drug addict. Or she was a drug addict. She might still be, I don't know."

Tears dripped down Beth's cheeks, and his stomach wrenched. Shit. What had he done?

She wiped her face with the sleeve of the flannel shirt.

"What else didn't you tell me? What else do I need to know?"

It felt as if she'd slapped him. He inhaled and took a step back, then gestured to the living room.

"If you come and sit down I'll tell you everything you want to know. I promise."

She crossed her arms tightly across her chest, but padded into the living room and perched in an armchair.

He sat on the coffee table directly in front of her. He couldn't bring himself to be more than a few inches away from her.

She curled in on herself and watched him, waiting.

"Angela is the cousin of the drummer for Thorny Lemon. She failed out of college and followed us on tour. I slept with her a few times, and we used condoms, but one of them must have broken. Next thing I knew, she was pregnant."

Shame filled him. When he said it aloud he sounded so careless and irresponsible. And it only got worse.

"I quit the band and we both moved back to Shepherdsville and got an apartment. She wasn't a drug addict when I met her. I swear to you. I'd seen her smoke marijuana, but nothing heavy or hard core. And I never saw her use when she was pregnant, not once."

He dropped his head into his hands. At least he could take comfort in that. He'd gone over it a million times, and he really, truly believed she'd been clean during the pregnancy. It was afterward, when the mundane, day-to-day life in Shepherdsville with a baby set in, that she'd succumbed to her addiction.

"I adjusted well enough. Being on the road had gotten old

and while I missed the music, I didn't miss traveling constantly and all the crap that came with it. But Angela had a harder time. She was the same as me, she'd never felt like she fit in in Shepherdsville. And then she was back with a baby, but she hadn't had any time to sort of find herself or explore the world. As far as I can tell she just cracked."

Anguish filled him. How could she have looked at Mabel and felt dissatisfied? True, the two of them had fought constantly. But why hadn't Mabel been enough to make her want to stay clean? It was beyond understanding.

Beth leaned forward, her eyes filling with sympathy, and his heart lifted. Beth would understand. She had to understand. He couldn't lose her.

"Why didn't you tell me? You let me think she was dead." Her face twisted, and his chest ached with fresh pain.

He clenched his fists. "I don't know. I really don't. I'm an asshole and I don't have any kind of excuse."

His heart pounded. The few times she'd asked about Angela, Beth's face had been so sweet, so sincere. He hadn't been able to stand the thought of ruining that. He hadn't wanted to see the way she'd look at him when she learned the truth.

"I guess I was afraid you'd look at me differently."

Her face scrunched. "Differently how?"

Like the way she was looking at him right now. Only he'd been the one to do this. He'd been the one who'd destroyed her faith in him.

"Like I'm a shitty, irresponsible father. I didn't want you to see me as the hard-partying enabler Angela's parents thought I was. I wanted you to believe in me."

"I did believe in you!" She jumped from the chair, her eyes red and her face stormy. "I always believed in you! You're the one who didn't believe in me. You didn't trust me with the truth."

She bolted to the hall and grabbed her purse, then flung the door open. "I can't be here right now. I need to think. By myself."

His muscles tensed as he leaped to his feet. He had to go after her, had to make her understand.

But she held up a hand to stop him. "You need to let me go." Her voice was steely.

He stopped short, his feet rooted to the spot. He watched, helplessly, as she slammed the door behind her.

Then he slumped into the wall and dropped his head into his hands. He'd ruined everything.

CHAPTER TWENTY

Beth paced along the beach, the sand coating her bare feet. The lighthouse and the moon illuminated her footprints in the dark as she trod back and forth.

How could he? How could he have lied to her, for all that time, about something this important? No matter what he said, there was no excuse. She'd deserved to know. Instead she'd spent months tiptoeing around his supposed grief, trying to reassure him that she understood her place in his life.

Shit. She kicked at the sand. The least he could have done was prepare her for the possibility that his long-lost ex-girlfriend might show up on the doorstep. As a freaking courtesy or something.

His secret changed everything, but not for the reasons he thought. She'd seen him perform with Thorny Lemon. She knew that he and his bandmates had a reputation as angry and edgy, irresponsible and reckless. But she also knew Griffin, and he wasn't any of those things. Whoever Griffin had been before, quitting the band and having Mabel had changed him. And she loved the person he was now.

Her breath grew tight in her chest. The details of his relationship with Angela didn't change the way she saw him, but the fact that he'd lied to her did. He'd let her live in a bubble of anxiety, unsure of her place in his life with Mabel.

A tiny part of her had felt guilty, as if she were stealing Angela's role in her family. She'd thought, if Angela had still been alive, she would have been the one to talk Griffin into Mabel's first sleepover, and if Angela had been alive, she would have been the one Mabel cried for as she threw up at school. Instead, Beth had been the one to do both of those things and hadn't felt fully entitled to do them.

Anger burned through her. The guilt and anxiety she'd felt were based on a lie. She'd never been stealing anyone's family.

And Griffin had let her go through that for no reason.

Her phone buzzed, and she fished it out of her pocket, staring at the illuminated screen in the darkness. The number had a local area code, but she didn't recognize it off the top of her head. It was probably a muffin order.

She eyed it, debating. She didn't want to talk to anyone right now, not even Kate or Ainsley. Her head was too mixed up. But if it was a business call she couldn't just ignore it.

"Hello?" She answered right before it went to voice mail.

"Is this Ms. Beverly?" A man's voice was on the other end.

Ms. Beverly. So it was work related.

"This is."

"Ms. Beverly, this is Fred Gallantry. I wanted to get in touch with you regarding my business proposal."

Frustration flared inside of her. She wasn't in the mood to deal with him or his offer.

"Mr. Gallantry. Yes, Griffin told me about your proposal. I need some time to think it over."

He sighed impatiently. "As you know it's a very fair offer, and I was hoping to have a decision by the end of the week."

Her heart rate sped. The end of the week? She had only five days to make one of the biggest business decisions of her life?

"Could I have more time? I need to…" she groped for a good excuse, "run some numbers."

She'd be stupid to turn down so much money, and yet, the whole thing felt wrong.

He chuckled. "Ms. Beverly you and I both know that my offer is more than sufficient to cover any overheard or investments you have. Simply put, there is no way you have any outstanding debts that would account for more than one hundred thousand dollars."

The back of her neck prickled. Regardless, it was her decision, and she didn't appreciate being rushed.

"I'd still like more time."

There was a long silence.

Her confidence grew. Why did he want her muffins anyway? A hundred thousand dollars was a lot of money, especially for muffins.

"Mr. Gallantry, would you mind telling me why, in particular, you want to buy into my business?"

He didn't hesitate. "Economics of course. Your muffins are the most sought-after muffins in Belmont. There's even a Facebook page to track the day and location of delivery as well as the precise time, so people can line up before they sell out. There's an exclusivity, a reputation of good taste associated with your muffins. It's not your business I want, Ms. Beverly, it's the value of your brand."

She paused in her pacing and thought. *Reputation of good taste.* What did that even mean?

Then it pinged. She laughed out loud. The thing he wanted from her, from her business, was something he could never buy. She was her brand. Her flighty nature, the whimsy that went into her products, her disinclination to expand production. Those weren't strategic business decisions or a carefully cultivated brand. They were just who she was. And he could never buy that.

"I'm sorry to disappoint you, Mr. Gallantry, but I'm not interested."

He cleared his throat loudly. "I assure you, Ms. Beverly, that one hundred thousand dollars is more than fair. Exactly what amount are you looking for?"

She sighed. Of course he wouldn't understand. "I'm just not interested in what you're proposing. It's not personal." She paused to think. How could she put this in terms he would understand? "It's business. But I do really appreciate the offer, and I hope you have a good night."

He sputtered unintelligibly.

"I do wish you the best of luck with your new business venture, Mr. Gallantry," she added before she stabbed the Off button with her finger.

There. As it turned out, she didn't need time to think it over after all.

One problem solved, but still her heart ached. What was she going to do about Griffin? She loved him, but how could she begin to forgive him?

She turned and started to walk back to Martha.

That was one decision she couldn't make tonight.

* * *

Griffin sat at the kitchen table as the full mug of coffee in front of him grew cold. He hadn't been able to sleep all night and his stomach was twisted in knots. This was all his fault. He'd created one hell of a mess, and he didn't know how to put it right.

He sighed and drummed his fingers on the table. To start with, he had to figure out the Angela thing. She might have terminated her parental rights, but she was still Mabel's mother, and Mabel deserved the chance to have Angela in her life.

He grabbed the crumpled slip of paper with Angela's number and dialed.

To his surprise, she answered on the first ring.

"Griffin?" Her voice was tense with anxiety.

"Yes. Beth said you stopped by, but I needed some time to think before I called."

She heaved a sigh. "Trust me, I understand. And I'm sorry if I upset your..." she trailed off.

His gut clenched. He couldn't talk about Beth right now, especially not with Angela. What had happened the day before was entirely his fault, but he couldn't shake the bitter taste

Angela's unannounced reappearance left in his mouth. If she hadn't shown up like that he would have had more time. More time to explain himself, more time to help Beth get used to the idea that Mabel was the product of a fling with a woman who had little interest in being a part of her life.

He cringed. He didn't want to imagine what Beth must think of him right now.

He gritted his teeth. "Angela, tell me what you want so we can discuss whether or not I think it's a good idea for Mabel. That's the only thing you and I need to talk about right now."

There was a pause. "Yes. Right. You're right. Um, I wanted you to know that I'm doing Narcotics Anonymous, and I'm doing really well on probation."

The muscles in his neck knotted. Coming from Angela, words and intentions didn't mean much. In the end he'd have to judge for himself whether she was clean and stable enough to be around his daughter.

"We have a lot of things we'll need to talk about, but May is going to wake up in a few minutes so I need to know why you're here and what you want, please." He struggled to keep his voice calm and level.

She sucked in a breath. "I know I signed away parental rights. I don't want custody. My parents aren't looking for custody. We know you're the best person to take care of Mabel, I just want to see her. No matter what, she's my daughter. And I've screwed up a lot but I will always love her, and I want a chance to know her."

His throat burned. He wanted that, too. Of course he wanted his daughter to feel loved and know where she came from. She didn't deserve to grow up with a mom-sized hole in her life.

"There would be rules." He wouldn't let Angela just waltz back into their life and play mommy. "Supervised visits at first. You have to take things slowly with her and let her get to know you. You can't just appear and expect her to accept that you're her mom. She might not be ready to treat you like a mom or call you Mom for a while, if ever."

He could hear his heart beat in his chest while he waited for her response. She had to agree. They would do this on his terms. This time around he had to do a better job of protecting Mabel.

"I understand." Another long pause. "Does she call her Mom? The woman? Beth?"

He nearly choked as emotion rose in his throat. Beth wasn't Mabel's mom and had never tried to be Mabel's mom. She was just…Beth. She loved Mabel, without labels or stipulations or qualifications.

His hands shook. No wonder she was so angry, so disappointed. She'd given her whole heart to them and he hadn't even had the decency to be honest with her.

"No." He didn't know if Angela was capable of understanding what the three of them, he and Mabel and Beth, had become. They weren't the most traditional family, but they were a family. God, he had to get her back. He didn't know if he could do this without her.

"I'm going to go check on Mabel. I'll talk with her today about meeting you and then I'll let you know. How long are you going to be in town?"

"I don't know. As long as my probation officer let's me, I guess. I kind of thought if things went well, maybe I'd stay for a while."

It took effort, but he let the comment pass without an inquisition. How long was a while? Where would she stay? What would she do? There'd be plenty of time to deal with that later. He had to take this one step at a time.

"Hey, Griffin?"

He gripped the phone tighter. "Yes?"

"Thank you." It was a whisper.

He clenched his eyes shut. They had to be clear on this one thing. "Angela, you're welcome. But I want you to know that I'm doing this for Mabel."

"I know. That's why I said thank you. You're a good dad. My parents were wrong about you."

His chest grew tight. They had been wrong about him. But he already knew that. "Thanks, Angela. I appreciate that. I'll talk to Mabel, and I'll keep you posted."

He clicked the Off button and pushed himself up from the table. Time to check on Mabel. She'd slept through the night and he'd taken her temperature several times. Her temperature had been coming down through the night, so with any luck she was feeling closer to her normal self.

He climbed the stairs and opened the door to her room. She sat in her bed, surrounded by a pile of stuffed animals.

"Hi, Daddy! Can I have my piggyback now? I'm hungry."

He walked to the bed and laid a hand against her forehead. Cool. Hopefully the fever was gone for good. "What do you want for breakfast?"

"Three pancakes, two eggs, four bacons, a muffin, and a banana."

Her appetite was back, another sign she had to be feeling better. Which meant she could have the full piggyback experience without his running the risk of being puked on. He sat on the edge of her bed and let her scramble onto his back. Then he stood up and gave a small horse-like kick.

"Hold on tight!" He galloped down the stairs and into the kitchen. He settled her into her booster seat, poured apple juice into a plastic cup, and placed it in front of her.

"Mabel, do you remember when we talked about where babies come from?"

He grimaced as soon as the words were out of his mouth. Real smooth. Not at all like the intro he'd rehearsed.

Mabel took a loud sip of juice, then smacked her lips. "Babies live inside mommies' bellies and then when they come out they grow up big like me!"

She slammed her glass down on the table and juice sloshed over the sides.

He forced himself to ignore the spill for the moment. "That means when you were a baby, you came from a tummy, too, right?"

Mabel paused and her eyebrows furrowed in thought. "Really? I came from a tummy?"

He quashed the urge to laugh. Sometimes it was hard to predict what would come out of her mouth.

"Yes. The tummy you came from belongs to a lady named Angela."

Mabel shrugged and took another sip of juice. "Okay."

His gut clenched. What now? He wished Beth were here. She'd know exactly what to say. She always did when it came to Mabel.

He took a deep breath. "She's visiting from Ohio for a little while, and she wants to meet you."

He watched Mabel's face carefully, searching for a reaction.

Mabel glanced up, a juice mustache on her upper lip. "Does she like to play?"

Relief washed over him. Mabel had friends with two daddies or one mommy or stepparents. Maybe this didn't feel that unusual to her.

He grabbed a napkin and wiped Mabel's face. "I'm sure she loves to play. And I bet she'll let you pick the games, too."

She nodded. "Okay. When's Beth coming? I miss her."

His muscles went taut. *I miss her, too.*

He missed her so much his chest physically ached. And he had not the slightest clue how to fix it.

"I don't know." His voice sounded choked, even to his own ears.

She frowned at him. "Well, you should call her, Daddy. And you should ask her to come over and play. And you should tell her that we love her very much, especially me."

His lungs constricted. If only it were that easy.

CHAPTER TWENTY-ONE

Beth stretched her arms over her head and yawned. She rubbed her eyes and stared at the clock on her bedside table. Seven a.m. How was it already seven a.m.? She'd slept fitfully all night and her eyes felt like sandpaper.

She pushed herself to a sitting position and grabbed her phone. A picture of her and Griffin and Mabel, arms wrapped around one another, grinning on the beach greeted her.

The anger ebbed out of her and was replaced by an ache that radiated through her entire body.

Where were they supposed to go from here? What happened now?

She loved Griffin and he loved her. She knew that down to her core. She loved Mabel and Mabel loved her.

But he lied. The memory sent a shard of pain shooting through her temple. He had lied. And now she knew the truth, but she still freaking loved him. Did that mean she was stupid? Crazy? Or just deluded?

Her eyes burned as fresh tears made trails down her cheeks.

She recalled the misery in his eyes when she'd turned and fled from his house. He hadn't meant to hurt her. She truly believed that. And he still loved her.

So what was the point of all this? What was she doing, sitting alone in her house, crying?

She jumped from the bed. She wasn't ready to give up. If he really loved her, if there was a chance they could be happy together, then she couldn't walk away.

She threw on a dress, brushed her teeth, and ran a comb through her hair. She couldn't go to him looking like a total ragamuffin. Then she grabbed her keys and raced out to Martha. She'd start at his house and keep looking until she found him.

* * *

A knock sounded on the door. Griffin stood up from the floor in Mabel's bedroom, where he'd been helping her illustrate her newest book Beth had written for her.

His limbs were heavy. It seemed no matter what he did, he couldn't get Beth out of his head. She hadn't just infiltrated his heart; she'd worked her way into every aspect of his life. He clenched his fists. He had to get her back. But how? A tree just wasn't going to cut it this time.

With a heavy sigh, he clomped down the stairs and peered through the peephole.

Beth. With her wild, curly hair and her compact body and

her dark, penetrating eyes. His heart thudded in his chest. She was here.

He wrenched the door open, but found himself frozen to the spot. His arms hung heavy next to his sides.

Every muscle in his body screamed at him to reach for her, to touch her and pull her close and yet he couldn't summon the courage to move.

What if she flinched away? He didn't think he could take that.

Then she was flinging herself at him, winding her arms around his neck and burying her head in his chest.

Overwhelming relief poured over him, making his throat tight.

"I'm so sorry." He wrapped his arms around her and whispered the words into her hair, inhaling deeply as her clean flowery scent enveloped him.

Her arms tightened around his neck. "I know."

His neck tensed. "I promise you don't have any idea how sorry I am. I've spent the entire morning wishing I could kick myself in the balls on your behalf."

She laughed then, and all the tension fled his body. Hope swelled in his chest. *A laugh. Thank God.* Maybe she really could forgive him.

She pulled back to look him in the eyes. "I want to be very clear that if you ever lie to me again, I will do something really awful to you. I haven't figure out what yet, but I will. And it will be terrible."

The corner of his mouth quirked upward even as his pulse skipped a beat. "I spent all night awake in my bed, alone, convinced I'd ruined things and lost you forever. I don't think you can invent a punishment worse than that."

She reached up to trail a finger along his jawline, and her throat bobbed as she swallowed. "I didn't mean to punish you. I just needed to think."

He lowered his forehead to hers, letting their breaths mingle together. "What did you think about?"

Tears gathered in the corners of her eyes, sending a sharp pain shooting through his side.

"I love you, and I don't want to be mad at you," she whispered.

He swallowed hard. "I hate it when you're mad at me. And I promise, from now on, I'm an open book. We can talk about anything you want."

"Anything?" She arched an eyebrow.

"Anything."

She shifted her gaze to the floor. "I thought Angela had died and there was some terribly hurt part of you that could never talk about her. And I guess I've been living in her shadow and worrying and wondering in some part of my brain how I stacked up and if I was invading her place or stealing her family."

A fat tear rolled down her cheek and his heart squeezed.

Regret rose in his throat. He pulled her closer and buried his head in her hair, lowering his mouth right next to her ear. His heart beat loudly in his chest. "In the spirit of full disclosure I have to tell you that you're incomparable. I have never met anyone like you in my life, and I have never wanted anybody the way I want you. I know that things are complicated and they're going to be complicated sometimes, but when it comes to you I want everything. And I actually feel like we can have it."

She nodded slowly, then tilted her head until her lips met his. Her kiss was soft but soulful. It seared his skin, as if she'd branded him.

Not that she needed to. He was hers. He'd been hers ever since he'd laid eyes on her.

She lifted her eyes to his. "I'm pretty sure we already have everything."

His blood pounded in his ears. She was here, home and in his arms. Yeah, he was pretty sure she was right.

EPILOGUE

Two Months Later

Beth and Griffin lay tangled in the sheets together, the last rays of sunset filtering through the window. Griffin wrapped an arm around her waist and pulled her closer, inhaling her scent. Angela would drop Mabel off from visitation in an hour, and he still had something he had to ask Beth. Looking down at her serene expression, he couldn't bring himself to wake her. She was exhausted from running her new studio.

She'd leased a location close to the theater where she taught classes. The new place had a professional-quality kitchen where she could bake muffins. In the main space she had one station set up for sewing and another for editing and polishing the children's books she and Mabel continued to crank out. They'd already self-published the first one on Amazon.

He pushed himself up onto the pillows and trailed a hand down Beth's bare arm. Happiness filled him to bursting. He was proud of her, proud of them. She was forging her own path and pursuing the things that made her happy. The same way he'd managed to run Little Ray and still make time for music. Their life and its trajectory weren't meant to be traditional. They were supposed to live outside the box.

Which left just one thing still missing.

She snuggled closer to his naked chest, and her eyelids flickered open. "Did I fall asleep?"

Blood pounded in his ears as he placed a kiss on her temple. "Yes, but that's okay. You had a long day. Go back to sleep."

She let out a delicious little murmur. "But there's a naked man in my bed."

He chuckled, his heart thudding louder. "Actually, it's my bed."

He ran a hand through her curls. "Which reminds me of something I need to talk to you about."

She propped up on her elbow and the sheet fell open to expose one naked breast.

He began to harden. He fisted his hands and searched for a few more seconds of self-control. "I think you should move in with me."

Her eyes went wide.

He rushed to continue. "You and me and Mabel. Plus Black Kitty of course, we make a good family."

A smile curled over her lips.

"Plus. I'm selfish. I like having you in my bed at night."

Then he couldn't take it anymore. He reached with one hand to cup her bare breast and lowered his mouth to hers, slipping his tongue inside.

She rolled onto her back, opening herself to him.

"You can take some time to think about it of course." He slipped one hand between her legs.

She mewled and arched up against him. Her breath was ragged in his ear. "Yes, my answer's yes."

With a self-satisfied smile, he lowered himself on top of her. It was exactly the answer he'd been hoping for.

Acknowledgments

To my agent, Dawn Dowdle, for encouraging me to turn *The Wedding Date* into a full-fledged series. Beth and Griffin wouldn't have gotten their happily-ever-after without you. To all of the writers at Blueridge Literary Agency, for your words of wisdom, encouragement, and advice. I learn something new from you every day.

Huge thanks to my critique partners, Jules Dixon and Ekaterine Xia. Katje, you're brutal and I need it. Jules, you're my marketing guru and always manage to walk me through things that seem impossible. I marvel at your energy.

To my editor, Michele Bidelspach, for always catching the thread of my ideas and helping me pinpoint where my characters are trying to take me. I'm so grateful for your vision, especially when mine is blurry. And to Jessie Pierce for always answering my emails quickly, no matter how crazy the question or how minor the concern.

Thank you to all my awesome new co-workers for your enthusiasm and encouragement. You make my days brighter.

Huge thanks to my husband, Dan, for picking up the slack when I crawl into the writing cave, and making sure I'm always fed. You're an inspiration. Thanks to you, I know what it is to have real, lasting love, and I will never take that for granted.

Event planner Ainsley Sloan spends her days creating perfect weddings for her clients and her nights wondering if she'll ever find her own happily ever after. So when her friend—and total man-whore—Ryan Lawhill starts making her skin tingle and her heart race, she's determined to shut it down. The last thing she needs is another broken heart. But when these opposites attract, can true love ignite?

Look for the next book by Kelly Eadon, available in March 2017. A preview follows.

CHAPTER ONE

Ryan Lawhill straightened his bow tie one last time, then raised his fist and knocked on the apartment door.

A few seconds later, it swung open. Ainsley stood on the other side, her blond hair twisted at the nape of her neck and her slim body encased in a sparking green gown.

Dark circles underlined her blue eyes, which were rimmed by red eyelids.

His chest ached. For the briefest of seconds, he was overcome with the urge to wrap her in his arms and crush her to him.

Then her gaze dropped to his blue, Converse sneakers, and her eyes narrowed. "You cannot wear those to a black-tie party."

And just like that, the feeling passed. He was wearing a tuxedo, which he'd rented especially for their friends Kate and James's engagement party. That meant he could wear whatever shoes he wanted. Plus, his Converses were sharp.

He rolled his eyes. "They match my bow tie. Besides, is that any way to talk to your Knight in Shining Armor? Your just-for-the-night Prince Charming?"

Kate had been very clear about his assignment for the evening: Protect Ainsley from party guests who wanted to gossip about her newly single status or rehash her breakup. Ainsley's boyfriend, Scott, had boarded the plane and moved to Hong Kong only forty-eight hours earlier. Without her. It was a fresh wound, and the Fallston crowd could be ruthless when they sensed blood in the water.

Which was another reason he'd worn the Converses. He'd give those uptight society types something else to talk about.

One side of her mouth quirked upward. "If you're my Prince Charming, even just for one night, my fairy godmother and I need to have a serious talk."

He lifted one hand to his heart and staggered back, feigning a mortal wound.

He glanced at her from the corner of his eye and caught her smiling. *Success!* Ainsley had a beautiful smile.

He straightened up and held out his arm. "Your chariot awaits, m'lady. She's a hell of a lot better than a magic pumpkin, too, if I do say so myself."

She hooked her arm through his. "On that point, I'd agree with you."

He grinned. His Mustang was sexy. Everybody knew it.

He punched the button to the elevator. They stood for a moment, waiting in silence. He let his gaze travel through the hallway. Over the plush carpet with intricate diamond patterns. Up to the detailed crown molding and the custom framed paintings on the wall.

He didn't want to know how much her rent was. And for what? To live in the Point? In a luxury building where every unit looked exactly the same?

No, thank you.

The elevator pinged its arrival and when he glanced back at Ainsley he saw tears crowding the corners of her eyes.

Shit. Hell. Damn.

His stomach clenched. He didn't do crying women. They triggered his urge to flee far, far away.

He gritted his teeth and tugged gently on her arm, leading her into the elevator. When she was safely inside, he pushed the button for the lobby.

"We don't have to go, you know." He blurted the words.

She dropped her chin and stared at her sparkly gold sandals. "We do have to go."

His spine tensed. "No, we don't. Kate didn't even want this party. If you'd rather go somewhere else or do something else, she'd understand completely."

He racked his brain. "I bet if I looked it up on my phone, I could find a club with male strippers."

Strip clubs always cheered people after a breakup, didn't they? Not that he'd ever gotten serious enough with a woman to find out firsthand.

She made a strangled noise in the back of her throat, then giggled. "I feel obligated to inform you, for the sake of all women, that we prefer our therapy in the form of chocolate and shopping. Although sometimes Magic Mike does hit the spot."

He shrugged. Hey, at least he'd tried.

She frowned. "And we do have to go. I promised Kate. Besides, my parents will be there. Along with everyone I grew up with and everyone I know. If I avoid it, they'll only talk more. I have to hold my head high and just get through it."

He swallowed a sigh. He'd never get that scene. Where was the fun in constantly worrying what other people thought of you?

He reached for her hand and squeezed it. "All right then. If we're actually going to do this, we need to come up with a special code word. Something that signals the need for immediate escape and rescue."

She raised an eyebrow at him. "For you or for me?"

He slanted her a look. Sure there'd be half a dozen women he'd hooked up with over the past year. But he could handle them. He wasn't the one who needed a bodyguard.

She wrinkled her nose. "I suppose 'strippers' would be an inappropriate safe word for the occasion."

His pulse sped. *Safe word?*

A strand of blond hair fell across her face, and he reached to tuck it behind her ear. Her eyes flicked up to meet his and suddenly his throat went dry.

He swallowed hard. "Why not? I have faith that you could work that into a conversation. In fact, I'd love to see you do it."

Her eyes flashed. "I bet you would."

The elevator pinged as it reached the ground floor and the doors slid open.

* * *

For the briefest of seconds, as she'd looked up into his deep-blue eyes and her heart thudded, she'd understood. She'd finally seen a flash of whatever compelled women to fall into his bed without the hint of anything more.

Then he'd given her that wolfish grin. "Personally, I'd love to see how the ladies who live at the Point react to the mention of strippers. Or does excessive plastic surgery prevent them from having facial expressions?"

And just like that, the feeling passed. He could make fun of her world as much as he wanted, but what people thought did matter. Belmont was a small town, Fallston was a small private school, and the Point was an exclusive neighborhood. She couldn't help it. She'd always cared what they thought of her and she probably always would.

With a huff, she strode out of the elevator ahead of him.

He could pretend all he wanted, but he needed her just as much as she needed him. Ryan had slept with half of the twentysomething women who lived in the Point. She'd protect him from scorned, disappointed lovers, and his presence as her date would allow her to save face.

She squared her shoulders. So what if she was almost thirty and still unmarried? So what if Scott had dumped her, leaving her to start all over? If anything, Kate and James were proof that love struck when you least expected it. They'd reconnected only six months earlier and were already engaged, partially thanks to her matchmaking abilities. Surely she could manage something similar for herself.

Behind her, the rubber soles of Ryan's sneakers squeaked on the marble floor.

"How do you walk so fast in those damn shoes?" he said. "If you're not careful, you'll break your neck."

She spun on her heel. The shoes put her a few inches short of eye level with him. Which was why she wore them. They helped her weed out any men who were too short to be marriage material. Even when desperate, she had requirements that couldn't be compromised.

His eyes sparkled mischievously. "So, safe words. Did you make a final decision yet?"

Her cheeks flamed, and she glanced over her shoulder to see if the uniformed doorman was listening. *Safe word.* Had she really said that? Talk about a Freudian slip.

She took a step in his direction and poked him in the chest with one manicured fingernail. "The safe word is 'commitment.' Because I want to see you work that into a conversation."

With that, she stalked out into the damp spring night, pulling her silk wrap tightly against her bare shoulders.

CHAPTER TWO

Ainsley's black silk clutch vibrated. She popped it open and pulled out her phone. That and a lip stain were the only two things she'd managed to wedge inside the clutch.

Kate's name flashed across the screen.

"Hello?"

"Houston, we have a problem." Kate's voice was a terse whisper.

Her pulse sped. The party started in an hour.

"What kind of problem?" Whatever it was, she had to fix it. Kate deserved for tonight to be perfect.

Kate inhaled sharply. "The dress doesn't fit."

Ainsley squeezed the phone so hard her knuckles ached. What did she mean it didn't fit? Kate had tried it on only a few days ago, when they'd picked the accessories.

"Of course it fits. You will make it fit."

There was a burst of hysterical laughter on the other end of the line. "I can't! My boobs are falling out."

Ainsley shook her head. Impossible. The satin gown had a high, draped neck, with a plunging back. The only place Kate's boobs could go was inside the dress.

"Send me a picture."

Kate's voice rose. "Of my boobs? I think not."

Ainsley took a deep breath. "A picture of the dress, not your boobs."

Ryan's head swiveled in her direction. With one hand, she pushed the side of his face until he faced the road again. The last thing they needed was a car accident.

Kate muttered an expletive. "I don't know how to get a picture of the dress without my boobs. That's the problem, the boobs won't go in the dress."

Silently, she cursed herself. She should have been there to help Kate get ready. She'd shown up at four, but Kate had sent her straight home with strict instructions to take a nap. Even her favorite concealer could no longer hide the dark circles under Ainsley's eyes.

"Don't panic." She spoke slowly, enunciating her words.

Kate was just nervous about the party. The only way to talk James's mother out of a five-hundred-person wedding had been to concede to a five-hundred-person-engagement party.

"Okay." Kate's voice quavered.

"Put the phone on Speaker and set it down. Then unzip the dress. Step out of the dress."

A few seconds passed.

"Now I'm naked, and I'm definitely not going to the party naked."

Ainsley chuckled. "I would never let you go to your own

party naked. Now find the little straps sewed inside, for the hanger, and hold the dress up."

The dress they'd chosen was silky and draped intricately so it hugged her curves. Kate could have easily slipped an arm through the wrong hole, causing the whole thing to hang wrong.

There was a rustling sound. "Okay."

"On one side the neckline will be high and on the other the neckline will be low. Very, very low."

"Yeah…"

"The high side covers your boobs. It goes in front. The low side doesn't cover your boobs, it goes in back. And I put double-sided dress tape in the front pocket of your garment bag so you can make absolutely sure everything that is supposed to be covered stays covered."

It was an industry trick she'd picked up years ago.

There was a whoosh as Kate let out a breath, followed by hysterical giggling. "Holy shit, I'm such an idiot."

Relief flooded Ainsley and she allowed herself to smile. "No, you're nervous, and someone should have been there to help you put on your dress. Except you ordered that someone to take a nap."

"Yeah, I did. Speaking of, did you finally get some sleep?"

Ainsley bit her tongue. No need to tell Kate she'd lain awake on her bed staring at the ceiling, going over the same damn questions. Why had Scott boarded that plane without her? Why didn't he want her?

Her stomach twisted, and she blinked back tears.

Not tonight. She was done wallowing.

"Uh-huh. Yeah. Ryan and I are already on our way over, so I'll see you soon. In your gorgeous dress, with your boobs in their proper place."

Kate sighed. "Thanks to you, I won't be naked. If you weren't already a bridesmaid, and my friend, I'd hire you to event-plan the shit out of my wedding."

Ainsley's chest grew tight, and she forced a laugh. That was her, the event planner who would never throw her own wedding. At this rate she should pull a Carrie Bradshaw and register for a crap-ton of expensive shoes.

She liked expensive shoes.

* * *

Ryan tossed his car keys to the valet. He glanced up at the massive, well-lit house and grinned. Some day, when his music-production company really took off, he'd buy a house like this. With the fancy columns out front and the floor-to-ceiling bay windows that spanned the entire first floor.

Only his house wouldn't be in the Point. And he'd throw parties full of musicians and artists and other creative types, not stuffy uptight financial brokers and insurance salespeople.

He bent next to the open passenger door and extended his arm to Ainsley. She rested her palm on his tuxedo sleeve and rose from the Mustang's bucket seat in one fluid motion. How did she do that? With her pointy heels and her long dress?

He shook his head. Women. She'd totter around on those shoes all night, but he bet she couldn't hike five miles in boots without complaining of blisters.

"You're here!" Kate flew out the front door, then skidded to a halt when she reached the top of the stairs.

Some women, he corrected himself. Kate in high heels resembled a baby elephant on stilts. James, who was clad in a tuxedo, stepped out beside her and rested a hand on the small of her back. He bent to whisper something in her ear, and she beamed back up at him.

Ainsley's hand on Ryan's arm tensed. *Shit.* It didn't matter how much she loved Kate and James, tonight was going to be hard for her. Even he could see that.

He cupped his left hand around his mouth and yelled, "Katie! Glad to see you figured out the boob situation. It sounded perilous, although I have to say, that would have made for one hell of an engagement party."

Next to him, Ainsley giggled, and the pressure of her hand on his arm lessened. *Good.*

Kate fixed him with a look, but the corners of her mouth twitched upward. "You're a pervert, Ryan Lawhill."

He waggled an eyebrow, and Ainsley dissolved into another round of laughter. *Mission accomplished.*

He and Ainsley climbed the stairs. When they reached the top, James pulled him into a back-slapping hug, while Kate embraced Ainsley. Then Ryan and Ainsley swapped places, and he gave Kate a quick squeeze.

"You look great," he said.

And she did. The dress had obviously been one of Ainsley's picks. It was long and dramatic, the fabric draping in ways that confounded him.

Good thing he wasn't the one who had to get her out of it.

Women's clothing should be sexy when worn and easy to remove. Was that so much to ask for?

Kate arched a brow. "Careful now, it sounds like you're finally coming to terms with your bridesmaid duties. And Ainsley has already claimed the role of bridesmaid style advisor."

He scowled. "For the last time, I'm not a bridesmaid. I'm a bridesman."

He grimaced. That sounded worse. "And I still haven't said yes."

Kate patted him on the shoulder as the four of them walked into the house. "Of course you'll say yes. Because you love me and you want me to be happy and you're one of my closest friends in the whole, entire world."

He sighed. Yup. She was right.

A sudden idea came to him. "So when I get married you'll be a groomsman? And wear whatever I tell you?"

Her eyes sparked. "Absofreakinglutely. When you decide to settle down, I will cram my ninety-year-old body into the tuxedo of your choice and use my walker to stand beside you at the altar."

He threw his head back and laughed. She had him there.

James raised one hand, in a pledge. "Ryan, I swear that if you choose to be a bridesman I will not let them put you in a pink tuxedo. Or purple."

Ainsley shrugged. "You didn't say anything about baby blue. I think a nice, light baby blue would be just the thing to bring out Ryan's eyes."

She reached to pinch his cheek, but he caught her wrist and took a step toward her.

Her eyes danced and his spine relaxed. All he had to do was keep her laughing for the rest of the night.

"Black tuxedo only. Promise me, Ainsley." His eyes held hers.

Her lips parted, sending a wave of heat through him. He took an abrupt step backward. *What the hell was wrong with him?*

He looked up to see Kate's and James's eyes fixed on them.

He quickly plastered a smile on his face. "I will accept my position as bridesman on three conditions. One, we find a new name for it because I'm not letting anyone call me that shit. Two, I wear what the groomsmen wear. And three, I get to help plan the bachelorette party but I'm going to the bachelor party. Because I've already started my research into strip clubs that feature male strippers."

James's mouth dropped open and Kate's face paled.

He pivoted on his heel and walked away, in pursuit of the bar. Let them chew on that for a while.

CHAPTER THREE

As Ainsley threaded her way through the crowd she stepped on a pair of men's dress shoes.

Immediately, she jumped back. "I'm so sorry."

When she lifted her gaze, her stomach sank. She found herself looking into a pair of ice-blue eyes whose shade matched her own perfectly.

"Ainsley." Her father gave her a curt nod.

"Father." Ainsley pecked him on the cheek.

Her mother was standing beside him and pulled Ainsley into a hug. "You look gorgeous, sweetheart. Just gorgeous."

Next to her, Ryan stepped forward and extended his open hand. "Ainsley's parents! Great to meet you."

Her father's gaze raked over him from head to toe. When he reached Ryan's blue Converses his upper lip curled slightly, but he took Ryan's outstretched hand and gave it one firm pump.

Ainsley cringed inwardly.

She shifted in her heels and tugged at one of her diamond

earrings. Her father fixed her with a stare, and she dropped her hand back to her side.

Where were Kate and James? Or Beth and Griffin? Anyone who could save them from her father's human-icicle impression.

"Nice party, huh?" Ryan grinned.

There was a long, painful pause.

"Yes, just lovely." Her mother's voice was quiet, as she sneaked a glance at Ainsley's father.

"I wonder when we'll have a reason to throw a party like this?" Ainsley's father fixed her with a cool stare.

Her tongue stuck to the roof of her mouth. Damn, she needed a drink. "There's always the Fourth of July. You can arrange a private fireworks display. I've planned a few parties that had them, and the guests are always impressed."

The muscles at the corners of her mother's mouth twitched. *See?* She nearly jabbed Ryan in the side. *Plastic surgery doesn't freeze your face.*

Ryan placed his hand on the small of her back. "Well, it was lovely to meet you both. I feel I'd be remiss in my duties if I didn't get my date a glass of champagne, and I'm sure you can't blame me when I say I'm reluctant to let Ainsley out of my sight. She's especially stunning this evening."

Her heart stuttered. Then he winked, and using the subtle pressure of his palm angled her body in the direction of the nearest bar. "I hope we'll have a chance to get to know each other better later."

She had only enough time to shoot her parents a quick smile before Ryan steered her across the room toward the arrangement of champagne flutes filled with bubbling liquid.

Ryan snagged two from the table and placed one firmly in her hand. "Bottoms up," he said and drained his glass in one long swallow.

She examined the flute. Why not? She followed suit, tipping the glass back and letting the cool liquid tickle her throat.

Ryan took the empty glass from her hand and replaced it with a full one. "Since I'm the designated driver, you definitely need another one of these. So, do you have brothers or sisters?"

She sipped this glass more slowly. "One sister."

Younger. And engaged, of course. Suddenly the champagne tasted bitter. She wanted this, the party and the engagement and everything that came with it, so badly it made her chest ache.

It took effort to swallow the champagne. "Why?"

He shrugged. "Your dad strikes me as the kind of guy who'd eat his young. You know, like a hamster or something."

She burst into laughter, waves of mirth rolling over her.

When she finally caught her breath, she looked into his blue eyes. Not cold like her father's, but clear and confident. Somehow warm.

Her grip on the champagne flute relaxed. Maybe her fairy godmother did know what she was doing, if only for tonight.